THE SHARDS OF EXCALIBUR

DOOR
into FAERIE

EDWARD WILLETT

Edited by Matthew Hughes
Cover and text designed by Tania Craan
Typeset by Susan Buck
Cover photograph by Gunjan Sinha
Printed and bound in Canada

Library and Archives Canada Cataloguing in Publication
Willett, Edward, 1959-, author
     Door into Faerie / Edward Willett.
(The shards of Excalibur ; book 5)
Issued in print and electronic formats.
ISBN 978-1-55050-654-9 (paperback).--ISBN 9781550506556 (pdf).--
ISBN 978-1-55050-891-8 (html).--ISBN 978-1-55050-892-5 (html)
     I. Title. II. Series: Willett, Edward, 1959- . Shards of Excalibur; bk. 5.
PS8595.I5424D65 2016   jC813'.54   C2015-908769-4
                                           C2015-908770-8

Library of Congress Control Number: 2015954155

2517 Victoria Avenue
Regina, Saskatchewan
Canada S4P 0T2
www.coteaubooks.com

10 9 8 7 6 5 4 3 2 1

Available in Canada from:
Publishers Group Canada
2440 Viking Way
Richmond, British Columbia
Canada V6V 1N2

Available in the US from:
Orca Book Publishers
www.orcabook.com
1-800-210-5277

Coteau Books gratefully acknowledges the financial support of its publishing program by: the Saskatchewan Arts Board, The Canada Council for the Arts, the Government of Saskatchewan through Creative Saskatchewan, the City of Regina. We further acknowledge the [financial] support of the Government of Canada. Nous reconnaissons l'appui [financier] du gouvernement du Canada.

Four nieces and a nephew – five books
This one is for Kamara

CHAPTER ONE

SPRING THAW

THE DROP OF WATER quivering at the tip of the icicle sparkled in the sun like a polished diamond. Wally Knight, heir to King Arthur, Companion to the Lady of the Lake of Arthurian legend, the doughty youth who had fought and defeated men twice his size, the intrepid lad who had journeyed all over the world on a dangerous quest to reunite the scattered shards of the great sword Excalibur, watched it with bated breath.

It fell, splashing to the gray-painted wood of the old farmhouse porch.

"Nine seconds!" Ariane announced. "I win! Again!"

"Well, you *are* the fricking Lady of the Lake, with magical power over fresh water," Wally grumbled.

"I assure you, Sir Knight, I need no magic to outsmart the likes of you." But Ariane smiled as she said it, and Wally grinned back.

They were sitting on the porch swing of the Barringer Farm Historic Bed and Breakfast in Cypress Hills, watching the snow melt and betting each other how many seconds would pass between one drop and the next falling from the slowly shrinking icicle above the steps.

Watching the snow melt was more exciting than it sounded, because melting snow meant the slough would soon thaw, and that would give them a body of water big enough for both of them to be submerged in. Not to go swimming – *ugh*, Wally thought, knowing what he knew of algae growth in stagnant ponds in summer in Saskatchewan – but because they needed that much water to materialize in after Ariane had used her magical power to transport them around the world via fresh water and clouds.

The snow melted faster than the ice thawed, especially in a pond small enough to have frozen solid, so there could be no using the slough yet. But the snowdrifts shrank daily and water dripped constantly from the icicles along the edge of the porch roof. It wouldn't be long.

And that meant soon they could travel anywhere they wanted.

Even though watching the snow melt *was* more exciting than it sounded, it still wasn't all *that* exciting, and Wally had actually had an ulterior motive in asking Ariane to sit out on the porch with him, and not the usual ulterior motive a boy might have for asking a girl to sit next to him on a porch swing. The fact was, he'd had an idea. A really great idea. But to make it happen, he had to get Ariane to agree it was a great idea, and sometimes Ariane wasn't convinced his great ideas were nearly as great as he thought they were. *And sometimes*, he thought, *to be perfectly honest, she's right. But not this time.*

Time to take the plunge. "Man, I can't wait to get out of here," he said, trying to sound casual, as yet another glittering drop fell from the icicle. That much, at least, he knew Ariane agreed with. The two of them had been cooped up in the farmhouse all winter, afraid to even venture into Maple Creek or Elkwater. The sorcerer Merlin – known to the general world as Rex Major, billionaire computer magnate – knew they had been using Medicine Hat as a staging area for trips around the country. That meant he must suspect they were in the area, and that meant they dared not show their faces, for fear of word somehow getting back to him. It wouldn't have to be from some gossiping busybody either; all it would take would be for someone to snap a photo of them with a phone connected to the Internet. Merlin's magic was a spider lurking on the Web, alert to any tiny vibration caused by Ariane's or Wally's presence.

Actually, being cooped up with Ariane, whom Wally could now officially, and rather unbelievably, call his girlfriend, might have been fun if not for the fact they were also cooped up with Ariane's mother, Emily Forsythe; Emily's sister, Ariane's Aunt Phyllis; and Phyllis's long-time friend, Emma McPhail, whose ideas of boy-girl propriety seemed to date back to Victorian England. But they *were* cooped up with that formidable female trio, and Wally had been feeing increasingly antsy. Spring feverish, even.

And, also rather unbelievably, he missed his family, dysfunctional and disjointed though it had become in recent months. He missed his dad, who was who-knew-where on business, no doubt accompanied by his recently acquired and much younger girlfriend. He missed his mom, also who-knew-where, most likely shooting a movie or a documentary. He even, God help him, missed his sister Felicia, though at least he knew where *she* was – living it up in Rex Major's Toronto penthouse condominium. Since she was also an heir of Arthur, and since Wally had rather thoroughly rejected Major's overtures to him – escaping that same condo, knocking one of Major's guards on the head, hacking Major's email, and stealing several thousand dollars from one of Major's bank accounts – Major had her tucked away for future use.

Like Ariane, Major/Merlin had two of the shards of Excalibur. Whoever was first to find the final piece, the hilt, would be able to claim the whole sword. And if that were

Merlin, Flish would – although Wally had a really, really hard time picturing it – wield Excalibur at the head of his armies. *Probably while wearing a designer dress and carrying a really expensive handbag in her free hand,* he thought.

Wally never would have believed almost five months could pass without some new development in the quest he and Ariane had been given last fall by the Lady of the Lake, but every day he asked her, "Any sense of where the hilt is?"

And every day she said…

Well, no, he hadn't asked her today. So now he did.

She sighed. "No, nothing. I keep hoping, with spring arriving, that maybe water will start running and come in contact with it, wherever it is, but…"

"It could be in the southern hemisphere again, anyway," Wally pointed out. "Antarctica, even."

"Yes, I know." She shook her head. "At least we know Merlin doesn't have it yet, either. My shards are still safe." She touched her side. She'd taken to wearing both of the shards against her skin, instead of just one, so they were always ready if she needed them. Even though she couldn't use the power of both of them together unless Wally was also touching them. Apparently, the sword liked him. Or liked the fact he was an heir of Arthur anyway.

Which was kind of cool, except, since Felicia was also an heir of Arthur, she could make the same connection for Merlin. And Merlin had his own powers, the extent of which they had only an inkling. Which had made it even more dangerous for them to venture into public anywhere close to their winter hideout.

But as the winter wound to its close, Wally had begun to think about the freedom they would gain with the melting of the ice. And that, combined with missing his family, and his general stir-craziness, had given him the great – well, seemingly great – idea he was about to bring up.

Another drop of water fell from the icicle.

"By Mother's Day, the pond will have melted," he said tentatively.

"By long before that, I hope," Ariane said.

"But by then for sure."

Ariane shrugged. "Probably."

"So…" Wally reached out and caught the next drop, cold against his palm. "Have you thought about what you might do for Mother's Day?"

"Um…no. Why?"

Wally could hear the confusion in her voice, but rather than look at her, he gazed out over the still-snowy fields into the blue distance. "I'm…thinking about my mom."

A pause. "You miss her?"

Wally nodded, but still didn't look around because he seemed to have something in his eye. He blinked to clear his suddenly blurry vision. "Weird, huh? She's been away more than she's been around the last few years, and she wasn't all that…involved, even when she *was* around. But I've watched you and your mom and…well, I keep thinking if you two can work things out, after everything she put you through, maybe…I should try to work things out with my mom, too.'"

"You could call her…" Ariane began, then stopped. "No, I guess that wouldn't be safe, would it?"

Wally sighed. "Not with Rex Major probably keeping tabs on all her calls. What if he traced it back here?"

"I could take you somewhere else and then you could call her – somewhere back east, or even in another country," Ariane offered.

"Yeah, I thought of that," Wally said. He turned to look at her at last; he'd blinked away whatever was making his eyes water. "But I really want to see her in person, and I couldn't arrange anything with her over the phone anyway. Even if Major wasn't actually listening in, he's probably Commanded her and Dad to tell him everything they hear from me. He'd set a trap, or use her as a hostage. You know how he loves hostages."

Ariane chewed on her lip. "So…any ideas?"

"One. If we can get somewhere where it's safe to use a computer, a library like we used when we were looking for your mom, I could check out her production company website. Sometimes she lists her current project and where she's going to be filming. Then we could go there and I could surprise her."

"On Mother's Day."

Wally shrugged. "If it worked out that way."

Ariane leaned over and kissed him on the cheek. He grinned, and touched the spot. "What was that for?"

"For being an incurable romantic," she said. "All right, let's do it. As soon as the pond is ice-free."

Wow, he thought. *I guess it really* is *a great idea!*

The pond took two more weeks to melt, during which time they discussed with the grown-ups where they might safely go. Emma suggested Weyburn. "Fine public library there," she said. "And there are any number of hotel pools to choose from, plus a public pool."

"Weyburn it is," said Ariane.

On a fine sunny day a few days later they stood in their swimsuits in the upstairs bathroom of the bed and breakfast, Ariane carrying a waterproof backpack with their clothes inside it. "Ready?"

"Ready," Wally said, though he wasn't really – the whole dissolving-into-water-and-materializing-somewhere-else thing *still* freaked him out. It was even worse this time, since it had been months since their near-disastrous excursion to Cacibajagua Island in the Caribbean. But he held on tight to Ariane's hand all the same, and a minute later they were in a hotel swimming pool in Weyburn, at the bottom of a waterslide. They surfaced and climbed out as if they'd just been swimming. There was no one else in the pool, but even if there had been, it wouldn't have mattered much. People were way more willing to believe the two teenagers who had suddenly appeared in the pool had been there all along and had somehow just been overlooked than that they'd materialized out of nowhere.

Go figure.

Ariane ordered the water off their bodies, they went into their respective bathrooms to change, and then they headed off on foot toward the Weyburn Public Library. A bit of a hike, but the weather was nice and at least they were somewhere other than Barringer Farm.

"What's that?" Ariane asked as they crossed a bridge over the Souris River. She pointed to the south, where a round white tower with a steep, conical roof and small windows down its sides rose on a hill.

"It's a hill," Wally said helpfully. "I know we don't have very many of them in Saskatchewan, but –"

She swatted his arm playfully. "I mean, what's that tower thing? It looks like a lighthouse. Or something Rapunzel might have lived in."

"It's an old water tower," Wally said. "There used to be quite a few in Saskatchewan that looked like that. I don't know how many are left – I know there's one like it in Humboldt." He grinned at her. "Looks like one thing, but it's really something very different. Just like you – after all, *you* look like an ordinary teenage girl –"

"Ordinary?" Ariane said, dangerously.

"Um…I mean, *you* look like an incredibly beautiful and talented teenage girl," Wally amended, "and yet in reality you're the heir to the Lady of the Lake."

"Yeah," Ariane said. "Fat lot of good it's done me for the last few months while everything's been frozen." She shook her head. "What if we *never* figure out where the hilt of Excalibur is? It's already been months. Maybe it's lost forever. And if it is…what will that mean? Will we have to hide from Merlin for the rest of our lives?"

"We can't," Wally said. "Sooner or later he'll find us."

"So what will we do?"

Wally said nothing. In the middle of the bridge he stopped and stared down at the little river, still swollen from the spring melt. "I don't know," he said at last. "Run away, I guess. Hide out wherever we can, for as long as we can."

"What kind of future is that?" Ariane said.

Wally said nothing, because the answer was obvious – a very grim one.

And it wasn't just he and Ariane who would have to hide. Rex Major had already taken Aunt Phyllis hostage, and Ariane's mom, once; he'd do it again in an instant. Wally figured the only reason he hadn't tried to use Wally's parents as hostages was because he needed Felicia's cooperation, and as much as his sister had become…whatever she had become…in the last while, he still believed she would rebel if Merlin threatened her parents.

Of course, he would have hoped she'd have rebelled when Rex Major threatened *him*, but she'd left him possibly dying or dead on the side of a hill on Cacibajagua Island after Merlin had called lightning down on him – well, not *on* him, obviously, but darned *close* to him – in order to claim the fourth shard for himself.

He turned away from the river and gave Ariane his best grin, hoping she couldn't see how forced it was. He was as tall as – no, make that a little taller than – she was now, his somewhat delayed adolescent growth spurt having set in in earnest about the time all these adventures had started in November. Sometimes he wondered if the sword's magic had spurred it along. "We'll do what we have to," he said. "Whatever it takes. Like we have, time and time again."

Ariane sighed. "In other words, you don't have a clue."

His grin widened, and now it was genuine. "Exactly."

CHAPTER TWO

MOTHER'S DAY

THE WEYBURN PUBLIC LIBRARY proved to be an interesting building, with a central part flanked by two wings, all three sections' curving roofs held up by pale blue pillars, topped by a crisscrossing network of support beams made of golden wood. Inside it was airy and full of light and, of course, books. But much as Wally liked books – and he *really* liked books – the only things he'd had time for at public libraries recently were the free computer terminals. Here, they stood just inside the door, not far from the main desk. The white-haired lady on duty gave them both a friendly smile as they came in. Wally smiled back, but he made sure he sat down at a terminal that had its back to the desk, so she couldn't see what he was looking up.

He also took a quick look around for security cameras. He knew Rex Major could sometimes access images from them – it was an image from just such a camera, mounted in a convenience store in Carlyle, Saskatchewan, that had revealed to both Major and Wally that Ariane's mother was still alive.

He called up his mother's production company. "Knight Errant Pictures?" Ariane said, reading over his shoulder.

"Yeah," he said. "I think she'd change it if she could, since that's her married name, but she's kind of stuck with it."

"Oh," Ariane said. Then, "What's her maiden name?"

"MacPhaiden," Wally said. "She comes from a long line of Scots."

He'd been clicking around on the site as he spoke, reaching *Current Projects; Shooting Schedule.* He blinked. "Well, that's a coincidence."

"What?" Ariane leaned closer to the screen.

"She's in Scotland. Shooting at a place called Castle MacPhaiden."

"An old family residence?"

"Maybe. I don't know much about our family history."

"What's the project?"

"Probably some low-budget fantasy flick. Scottish sword and sorcery." He grinned. "Polearms and porridge. Halbards and haggis."

"Wally..." Ariane growled.

"Sorry," Wally said contritely. He clicked on the project link, and blinked again. "Huh. Wrong again. It's something titled 'Family Legends,' and she calls it, 'a personal journey of discovery.'"

"Sounds like she's researching that family history you say you don't know much about," Ariane said. "I wonder if she'll turn up anything about King Arthur?"

"That'd be on the male side," Wally said automatically.

Ariane raised an eyebrow at him. "Would it?"

"Of course it –" Wally stopped. *Sexist much?* he thought. Sure, in Arthur's day boys came first when land and titles were inherited – what was the word for that, prima...primo...*primogeniture*, that was it. Although, come to think of it, the word itself just meant the firstborn inherited, it didn't specify the firstborn being male. But that had nothing to do with genetic inheritance, and – he'd bet – even less to do with magical inheritance, which clearly followed its own rules. After all, after so many generations, there should be hundreds or thousands – or maybe even hundreds *of* thousands – of "heirs of Arthur" or "heirs of the Lady of the Lake" floating around. Instead there appeared to be only him and his sister on the Arthurian side, and Ariane – and before her, her mother – on the Ladyian (Lakeian?) side. And the fact they'd both ended up in Regina, Saskatchewan, at the same school, and at the same lake at the same time on the same morning...that was far more than coincidence. The magic had been choosing its path since the days of the original Arthur. Presumably it had always been in *someone*, someone who could have wielded Excalibur had it been reforged, or someone who could have accepted the power of the Lady of the Lake had it been offered.

So why wasn't it? Wally thought, and was a little startled it was the first time he'd thought it. *Why didn't the Lady...um, "activate" one of her heirs before now? Merlin was imprisoned for centuries. Why not reforge Excalibur before he could even go looking for it?*

It might have been the first time he'd asked that particular question, but it certainly wasn't the first time he'd questioned whether the Lady of the Lake had told them the whole truth. *Maybe someday I'll get to ask her,* he thought.

Right. And I'm sure she'll tell me the whole truth and nothing but the truth when I do.

"You're right," he said humbly to Ariane. "Whatever Flish and I have inherited from King Arthur could have come down through the male *or* female side. The fact it ended up in someone named Knight may have just been coincidence."

"Or Excalibur's idea of a joke," Ariane said darkly.

Wally knew what she meant. Excalibur was clearly

more than a hunk of metal. It had communicated with both Wally and Ariane – mostly variations of "kill your enemies," so it wasn't exactly a wisecracking Disney side-kick sort of sword – but still, who could say just how sentient it was?

Maybe we'll find out if we ever get it put back together, Wally thought, and it wasn't a comfortable thought. He knew Ariane's mantra of "I control the sword, it doesn't control me," and he approved – but those were just words. Maybe just teenage bravado.

Just who *would* be in control once the sword was forged anew?

He shook his head. Hypotheticals were just that – hypothetical. "Whatever, this Castle MacPhaiden is where Mom's going to be on..." he checked the calendar, and grinned. "On Mother's Day. How perfect is that? I'll surprise her."

"I'm sure you will," Ariane said dryly. "So where is it, exactly?"

A quick Google turned up more information about the castle, which was far off the beaten paths in the Highlands of Scotland, and privately owned. It saw few tourists, although it had been used in a number of movies and TV series over the years. Wally skimmed the history. "Built in the thirteenth century...came into the MacPhaiden family in the fifteenth century when a wedding feast ended in the slaughter of the previous owners...said to be haunted by the murdered mother of the groom, who walks the battlements in a long white robe, wailing her anger and grief."

"I don't believe in ghosts," Ariane said.

"You didn't believe in magic until a few months ago," Wally pointed out.

Ariane laughed. "You've got a point. Maybe we should take some garlic, just in case."

"Um...that's vampires. For ghosts you use..." Wally

thought about it, and realized the only lore he had at his disposal had come from watching *Supernatural.* "Um...salt or cold iron?"

"Why does it have to be cold iron?" Ariane asked curiously. "Wouldn't hot iron work just as well?"

Wally laughed. "I don't know. That's just the way it's always described."

"Well, we've got the cold iron," Ariane said. "Two shards of Excalibur. You can pack a saltshaker, too, if you want." She straightened. "So you really want to do this?"

Wally went back to the Knight Errant Pictures website, and called up the publicity shot of his mother. It was a few years old, old enough that he remembered when she'd brought it home to show the family. He'd been eleven and Felicia had been just-turned fifteen and his best friend. It had been a wonderful year...

...and it had been shortly after that his family had started to fall apart.

Now the four of them were scattered all over the world.

He couldn't do anything about patching things up with Felicia. He'd at least spoken to his father. But his mom...it had been months since he'd even heard her voice.

"Yes," he said. "I really want to do this."

Ariane nodded. "Well then," she said. "Let's all celebrate Mother's Day in Scotland."

Wally blinked at her. "All of us?"

She grinned. "Why not? It's spring, we've got no lead on Excalibur, we're going stir-crazy. I can take everyone to Scotland...it might take a couple of trips, but I can do it. We'll have some fun, and you can talk to your mother." She kissed him on the cheek. "It's my present to you both."

"Thanks," he said, as the computer screen turned strangely blurry. *They should replace it*, he thought.

They didn't have to go back to the hotel to travel

back to Barringer Farm, and there wasn't even any need to change into their swimsuits. They'd arrive in the slough, to be sure, but Ariane could order the water off of them the moment they climbed out, and hot showers and clean clothes awaited in the house. Which was important, since, although she could remove the water, whatever was *in* the water stayed on their clothes and there was a whole herd of cows that spent a lot of time down by that slough.

They went in search of a bathroom, their path taking them past a reading area with comfortable chairs and a few magazines scattered on low tables. Wally glanced down at one of the tables as they passed, and stopped dead.

Ariane took another step, then turned back inquiringly. "What?"

Wally pointed. "Look."

Ariane looked down at what had brought him up short. "Oh," she said.

Rex Major smiled toothily at them from the front page of a business magazine. *ENTREPRENEURS FOR EDUCATION* read the banner over his head, so he was clearly at some kind of gala charity fundraiser. And in the background, dressed in a low-cut slinky dress that sparkled in the lights, was Wally's sister, Felicia, slightly out of focus but still recognizable, and looking ten years older than her actual age of eighteen. "Seems to be enjoying herself," Wally muttered.

"Come on," Ariane said.

A moment later, after making sure no one was looking their way, they ducked together into one of the main-floor washrooms, Ariane turned on the tap, and they were on their way back to Barringer Farm.

Unfortunately, Ariane's grand plans for a mass outing to the Scottish Highlands didn't work out. Emma and

Aunt Phyllis both flat-out refused to come, making it clear they had no desire to experience Ariane-travel again, having survived it once. It was a sentiment Wally could appreciate, but it wasn't as if he had a choice. "It's only planes, trains and automobiles for me from now on, dear," Aunt Phyllis had said. "Besides, Emma and I have to get the place spic-and-span for the Barringers. They'll be back June first, you know."

So in the end, only he and Ariane and Ariane's mom convened in the upstairs bathroom at ten o'clock at night, water running in the sink. The odd departure hour had been necessitated by Wally's guess – though admittedly it was only a guess – that his mom and her film crew would show up at Castle MacPhaiden very early in the morning in Scotland. Since they were well past the equinox, sunrise was around five a.m. that far north...and there was a seven-hour time difference.

Which meant, of course, that Wally would probably be yawning his head off during any meeting with his mother, but there wasn't much to be done about that. *People who complain about jet lag have never experienced Ariane-lag*, he thought.

Ariane held out one of her two shards of Excalibur to Wally. The other, he knew, rested against her side beneath a tensor bandage, where this one would join it later, when it wasn't needed any longer. Supposedly Major couldn't just *take* them from her and make use of their power – she had to give them to him willingly, at least until he got the final piece, the hilt. But that didn't mean he couldn't get hold of them and hide them somewhere the teens would never be able to find them, if he somehow obtained one Ariane had left in a place she thought was safe but wasn't.

Wally took the proffered end of the shard in both hands. The piece of Excalibur didn't sing to him, as Ariane said it did to her, but he could feel its magic, like a vibration or a faint electrical charge, thrumming in the steel and in his fingers. The spark of magic he'd inherited from Arthur somehow activated the sword's own power – it seemed *pleased* that he was touching it.

"Hold on to me, Mom," Ariane said, and Emily wrapped her arms around her daughter. Ariane plunged her free hand into the running water, and the bathroom dissolved around them.

Almost at once, it seemed, they erupted into the cold water of a small lake – *loch*, Wally corrected himself. Castle MacPhaiden, recognizable from the photos of it on his mom's website, loomed off to the south, little more than a grey blob in the morning mist under a drizzling rain.

"Sorry about the weather," Ariane said.

"What?" Wally said in mock outrage. "Can't you control that, too?"

Ariane laughed. "Not yet."

Wally grinned. "Welcome to Scotland. This is the same kind of weather we had the whole week I spent in Edinburgh with my family a few years ago." He peered through the mist and rain at Castle MacPhaiden. It wasn't a very large castle, really just a large house – maybe "keep" was the right word – built behind a battlemented wall at the top of a cliff. The road running up to it passed by the loch, maybe a hundred metres away. They trudged across boggy ground over to the road, then stood on its crumbling pavement, stamping their feet to knock the mud off their shoes.

"Mom and I will go down to the village," Ariane pointed the opposite way from the castle. "We'll wait by the church for you at noon, if we don't see you before then."

Wally nodded. "Be careful," he said. "If anyone takes a photo of you, Rex Major could –"

"Take hours to get here," Ariane said. "Don't worry,

Wally. And good luck with your mom."

"Yes, good luck, Wally," Emily Forsythe chimed in. She smiled at him, and he was struck by how much her smile looked like Ariane's. "I'm sure she misses you more than you realize. She's going to be thrilled to see you. Wish her Happy Mother's Day for me. I wish I could meet her."

"Someday," Wally said.

But not today, he thought, as he turned and started the cold walk toward the forbidding grey castle. *Not while she's still under Merlin's Command to tell him everything she knows about Ariane and me.* He would have to be exquisitely careful in his choice of words to her, since he had to think she would give a word-by-word account to the sorcerer. He trusted *himself* to be that careful, but he didn't trust Ariane's mom. The fewer people who had to guard their words, the better.

Less than an hour later, he stood on the battlements of castle's wall, damp and dripping, stamping his feet to keep warm, watching the road, feeling like an ancient sentry awaiting the arrival of an invading army...and here they came at last, advancing on the castle under his mother's command.

Not that it was a very large army – a car and a van. And not that he could be entirely certain his mother was in either of them – it could just be a vanguard of the camera crew. But he didn't think so. His mom had always been a very hands-on filmmaker. She'd want to be at the location right from the beginning.

He realized belatedly that if he could see them they could potentially see him. So he ducked down behind the wall, sat on the cold, wet ground, and waited, his heart pounding in his chest.

Funny. He'd fought Merlin's thugs, been held at gunpoint by Merlin himself, flown halfway around the world on his own, swum to an island in the middle of a New

Zealand lake, and been almost struck by lightning on a Caribbean island – and yet this impending meeting with his mother scared him more than any of those.

The road curved around to the north of the castle, where a long drive led up the hill to the main entrance, out of his sight. It passed through a portcullis and emptied into a cobblestoned courtyard, with the keep on the east side and several smaller outbuildings to the west. These were probably originally stables and storerooms and now, it looked like, garages, although there were six garage doors. Who needed that many garages?

Maybe the owner collects cars, he thought. He knew the castle still belonged to a MacPhaiden. *A relative?*

Maybe his mom could tell him.

He heard the rumble of tires on the cobblestones, heard the sound of doors opening and closing. The castle seemed unoccupied. He'd approached it cautiously, but seeing the shuttered windows and the lack of smoke from the chimneys, he'd decided it was safe enough to take up his sentry position against the wall. He ran over to the keep and, keeping close to the wall – the tall, thin windows were still well above his head even when he stood upright – crept to the corner, and then crawled forward on all fours until he had a view of the courtyard through a screen of heather.

Wally saw his mother at once. Wearing jeans and a warm-looking woolen sweater, her long brown hair drawn back in a practical ponytail, she stood with her hands on her hips, talking to a man he recognized as a cinematographer she'd worked with before. "We'll set up in the Great Hall," he heard her say, and, to his astonishment, the mere sound of her voice made his throat constrict.

Getting sentimental in your old age, Wally. Is this what being fifteen is going to be like?

The camera-guy nodded, and went back to the van to help the rest of the crew – just one other man and a woman, both of whom, like the cinematographer, looked vaguely familiar – start unloading equipment and cables. Behind the van, a third vehicle, a big black Jaguar with tinted windows, rolled into the courtyard.

Meanwhile, his mom had turned around, and now she walked straight toward him.

Wally scuttled back and around the corner of the keep and stood up again, heart pounding harder than ever. He'd been wondering what would be the best way to reveal himself, and had imagined any number of scenarios – but not one that had him rising from the heather like one of the angry ghosts that supposedly haunted the castle. His mom might have a heart attack!

He stared across the open space between the keep and the wall, wondering if he could arrange to be casually standing on it when she came around the corner, as though he just happened to be sightseeing in the very place she had chosen to shoot a film.

And that was when the idea that had seemed so great back on the porch in Saskatchewan turned bad.

Very bad.

"Mom! Mom!"

Wally's head jerked around as he heard a new voice echoing around the castle courtyard.

Flish!

CHAPTER THREE

STORMING THE CASTLE

THE SMALL VILLAGE located just five kilometres down the road from Castle MacPhaiden had looked pleasant and picturesque in the pictures Wally had showed Ariane online in Weyburn, but those pictures had all been taken on a sunny summer day. On a grey and drizzly spring day, at 6:30 in the morning, it wasn't nearly as pleasant. Although Ariane grudgingly admitted to herself it could still be seen as picturesque, at least in a "What a great setting for a creepy *Doctor Who* episode involving alien invasion!" sort of way.

"I may not have thought this through very well," she said to her mother, apologizing yet again as they trudged into the town. She'd used a little of her power to keep them dry during the walk, but she didn't dare do that where anyone could see them and so now they were getting both cold and wet.

Mom laughed. "Ariane, stop apologizing. I'm just happy to be with you on Mother's Day for the first time in years."

Ariane swallowed hard at that, and tamped down the little bit of residual anger that still tended to rise in her when she thought of how – and why – she'd been without her mom for so long. She understood now that her mother had run away, after refusing the power of the Lady, to try to protect her daughter, to try to ensure Ariane wasn't drawn into the Lady of the Lake's quest to gather the shards of Excalibur and, more importantly, wasn't drawn into the crossfire of the feud between the Lady and her brother, Merlin – Rex Major. It had been a useless attempt, and all that it had accomplished had been to land Ariane in a series of foster homes and a series of schools – complete with a series of assorted bullies – but she *did* understand, and she had forgiven her mother.

Mostly.

"Well," Ariane said, "I think I see a coffee shop up ahead. At least we can get out of the rain."

The shop had just opened and the young woman behind the counter, who looked to be no older than Ariane and sported hair as red as Wally's – which was about as red as human hair could be – seemed more than a little startled to be entertaining Canadian tourists that early, but the coffee was hot and so were the sticky buns, and Ariane and her mom sat contentedly and watched the village come to life outside the rain-spattered windows.

For the life of her, Ariane couldn't have told anyone later what they talked about. All her thoughts were elsewhere, down the road and up the hill at Castle MacPhaiden, where by now, if all had gone as expected, Wally must have met his mother.

She'd promised they'd be waiting for him at the church at noon, but that still gave them – she glanced at the clock on the coffee shop wall and sighed – four and a half hours to kill.

She spotted some tourist brochures in a rack by the door, and grabbed one and brought it back to the table, only to discover that everything listed as being of interest was a several-kilometre drive away. The village itself apparently had little to offer except a pub with a few hotel rooms upstairs, a post office, a general store, a druggist's, the coffee shop, a bicycle repair shop, a petrol station, and the ancient church, which predated even the castle by a century.

The latter, at least, was open, and so after they'd lingered as long as they could in the coffee shop – the girl at the counter kept looking their way as if wondering when they would ever leave – they went back out into the rain and trudged down the cobblestoned street to the squat grey building. It didn't take long to tour its dark-stone-and-darker-wooden-beams interior. The stained-glass windows, installed in the fifteenth century, were supposed to be rather fine, but with the outside light so wan they looked as washed out and dull as everything else in the village.

It wasn't anywhere close to noon when Ariane and her mother stepped back out into the street – more like 8:30 – but as they hunched their shoulders against the rain again, she saw Wally at once, splashing through puddles toward them as though pursued by a demon – as she should know, because in her dreams she'd once *been* pursued by a demon, sent by Merlin to frighten her into giving up the quest.

He reached them and stopped, panting and dripping, his usual geeky T-shirt – today's showed a green sea monster above the words "Don't Mess With Nessie!" – clinging to him like a second skin.

"Did you see your mother?" Emily Forsythe said.

"Yes," Wally gasped out.

"And?" Ariane said.

He leaned over, hands on his knees, breathing hard. "I saw her, but I didn't talk to her."

Ariane blinked. "Why not?"

He raised up. "Because," he said, "Flish is with her – and so is Rex Major."

Ariane felt as if she'd been slapped. "What? How?"

"I don't know." Wally sounded almost angry. "I saw my mom arrive, she got out of the car, she was coming around the corner of the castle, I was going to let her find me there. Then another car drove up and I heard Flish yell, 'Mom,' and when I looked there she was – and Rex Major was getting out of the car she'd just pulled up in." No "almost" about it, Ariane realized – he *was* angry. "She managed to screw this up for me, too. She screws up everything."

"She didn't know you'd be here, Wally," Ariane's mother said. "She didn't do it on purpose."

Ariane frowned at her mother. Reasonableness from a grown-up at a moment like this was *always* irritating, but somehow grown-ups never seemed to grasp that simple fact. She looked back at Wally. "We should just get out of here, Wally. We can find your mother alone some other time, some other place."

Wally shook his head. "No, we can't," he snapped. "Don't you get it? Flish isn't here just because it's Mother's Day. She's here because she knows Mom is researching family history. And that means Rex Major thinks there might be something in that history that will lead him to the hilt."

Ariane frowned again, this time at Wally. "I know we kind of joked about your mom finding out something about King Arthur in your genealogy, but don't you think it's really a long shot?"

"Maybe it's not," Wally said. "If Major's here, maybe it's not a long shot at all. And even if it is, what if it's a long shot that pays off, and Flish gets information from Mom that points to the location of the hilt, and we don't? Merlin would have the last piece of the sword before we knew what hit us."

He had a point. "So what do we do?"

"We have to find out if Mom has learned anything yet." Wally's expression hardened. "And at the same time, maybe we can do something else."

Ariane stared at him. "What?"

"What if we could get Flish away from Rex Major?" Wally said in a low, intense voice. "We can't steal his shards from him, but what if we could steal his personal heir of Arthur? We know he needs her to use the power of the shards he has, just like you need me. Without her...well, he's too rich to be powerless, but at least he'd be less powerful *magically*. It might just give us the edge we need."

"You're talking about kidnapping your sister!" Ariane's mom exclaimed. She shook her head. "No. It's not only dangerous, it's illegal. I forbid it."

Ariane's anger flared up again, fed by the shards she carried, sure, but not originating with them. "Dangerous? As opposed to everything else we've done? And I'm sorry, Mom, but what gives you the right to forbid anything? You refused the power of the Lady of the Lake."

"Ariane!" Mom looked shocked, but Ariane turned her back on her.

"There's a pond just outside of town, much closer than the loch," she told Wally. "Wait for me there."

His eyes flicked from her to her mother, and he nodded. Then he turned and ran off.

"Wally –" Ariane's mom called, but whatever else she was going to say was cut off by Ariane grabbing her arm. She looked down at Ariane's hand, looked up at Ariane, and opened her mouth to protest –

– but a moment later she had no mouth, as Ariane took to the clouds.

She sped them back to Barringer Farm in minutes. They emerged in the slough, and she led Mom to dry land, ordering the water off of them as they emerged onto the weed-grown bank. Mom glared at her. "Ariane, just what do you think you're –"

"Sorry, Mom," she said. "But I need you safe. Happy Mother's Day."

And then she plunged back into the water and away.

No more than twenty minutes after leaving the steps of the church, she re-emerged in the pond on the edge of the village, to find Wally waiting for her as instructed. She waded out and wished herself dry.

"I'm sorry to ruin your Mother's Day outing," Wally said.

"It's okay," Ariane said. "It's a really, really boring town. Dull as dishwater. But trying to kidnap your sister? Now *that* sounds like fun." She grinned at him. She was only slightly joking. She and Flish had history, none of it good. Flish's gang of girls had bullied her in the school, tried to strip and shame her by the lake, and ambushed her on the tennis courts. She'd broken Flish's leg in that last encounter, and almost lost Wally's friendship as a result. She'd promised him she wouldn't hurt his sister again – but they could kidnap her without hurting her, couldn't they?

And besides, it was *Wally's* idea.

"What's your plan?" she asked him.

He shrugged. "Simple. We watch. We catch her outside. We run up, we grab her, we all fly away."

"To where?" Ariane said. "We don't dare take her to Barringer Farm. If she managed to get away or get a phone call out to Major…"

"We can't hold her prisoner indefinitely anyway," Wally said. "But if we can just get her away from Major so we can talk to her – so *I* can talk to her – then maybe…" His voice trailed off.

Ariane said nothing in response, but based on her experiences with Flish, she thought it a fool's hope to believe they could talk Flish out of her new, rich-celebrity lifestyle. Still, if they could hold her for even a few days, keep her away from Rex Major, and if they also had a lead on the hilt...

"You still need to talk to your mother," Ariane said. "You need to find out if she's learned anything about your family history that might actually help us."

"But how do I do that with Rex Major hanging around?" Wally said. "I'll bet you anything he's funding this shoot. There's no way I'll be able to convince my mom that he shouldn't hear us talking about what she's learned in her research."

Ariane chewed on her lip for a minute. "I think I have an idea," she said slowly. "If Rex Major sees me, but thinks I don't see him, he's going to think I've got a lead on the hilt. He's going to come after me to see what I'm up to. And he's going to bring Flish with him so he can use the shards' power if he needs to. I'll lead him on a wild-goose chase while you talk to your Mom. Then I'll disappear and double back. Major and Flish will come back to the castle, tails between their legs, you'll have learned whatever your Mom knows...and *then* we can grab Flish and run. How's that sound?"

"Vague," Wally said. "Very, very vague." He grinned as he said it, though. "But it just might do the trick. So...where do you show yourself that will draw Major's attention?"

Ariane had been asking herself that same question, and studying the valley. Something caught her eye, up the slope from the castle, a white trail – water, leaping over rocks down from a mist-shrouded summit. "Up there," she said, pointing. "He'll expect the hilt to be hidden in water somewhere, like every other piece has been. He'll think I'm looking for it in the stream. How can he resist?"

Wally followed her finger. "Could work," he said.

Then he looked back at her, face serious. "But be careful," he warned. "He can't kill you without destroying the sword – we *think* – but you know he'll *hurt* you without a second thought."

A warm feeling at Wally's concern turned to a hot flame of sword-driven rage in Ariane's heart. "The feeling," she snarled, "is mutual."

Wally nodded. "And don't hurt Flish."

"I won't, Wally," Ariane said. "I promised you I wouldn't, and I meant it."

"Good." Wally took a deep breath. "I guess that's our plan, then." He looked along the road to the old keep clinging to the top of its cliff. "Time to storm the castle."

The rain hadn't slackened as the day aged; if anything, it was raining harder, which made for miserable walking, since Ariane didn't dare use her power to keep them dry this close to Rex Major. On the plus side, though, it also made for poor visibility, which suited them while they tried to get back to the castle unseen, even if it didn't particularly bode well for Ariane's attempt to attract Major's attention. "I'll just have to start closer to the castle to be sure he can see me," Ariane said. "He won't catch me. But I'll bet he chases me."

It all seemed like a reasonable plan. But Ariane had once read a famous military dictum to the effect that no battle plan survives contact with the enemy, and as they began climbing the road to the castle, they proved that rule, because they made contact with the enemy long before they'd expected to – headlights glowed in the fog ahead, and they barely had time to scramble to the side of the road and crouch down in the ditch before a black Jaguar rolled by.

Wally jumped up and stared after it. "Rex Major was in that car," he said. "But not Flish."

Ariane had been too busy hiding to try to see who'd been

driving. She got to her feet and stood beside him, staring down the wet road at the disappearing red taillights. "You're sure?"

He nodded.

Ariane felt a thrill – and was also very glad she'd rushed her mother back to Saskatchewan, because if she'd left her in the village and Rex Major had chanced to see her as he rolled through, he would certainly have grabbed her. And if Major got hold of any of them again, he wouldn't make the same errors he'd made in the past. Rescuing her mom a second time would be far, far harder.

As it was…

"This may be easier than we'd hoped," she said. "Lead on, Macduff!"

"Actually, the quote is 'Lay on, Macduff,'" Wally corrected, but he led on all the same, especially after she swatted the back of his head. "Probably bad luck to quote *Macbeth* anyway," he added over his shoulder, and she laughed.

They hurried up the steep road toward the dark bulk of the castle, slowing as they got close to the gate. "Let's not be quite so obvious about it," Wally said. "While I was exploring this morning, I found another way in. Follow me."

He led her around the outside of the castle wall, along a narrow path with a terrifying drop on the left and the wet grey stones of the wall on the right. Ariane looked nervously down at the valley floor a hundred metres below. "I'm the Lady of the Lake, not a mountain goat," she said. "Is it far?"

"Not far," Wally said. "It's a tunnel through the wall."

"A tunnel? In a castle wall?" Ariane stared at the back of his head. "Isn't that a security risk?"

"Lots of castles have them," Wally said. "Originally it would have had a door sealing it. A postern gate."

"A what?"

"A postern gate. Sometimes when you're in a castle you want to be able to get out without opening the main gate, especially if there's, say, a hostile army camped outside."

"But what keeps the hostile-army people out of the postern gate?"

"It's locked and guarded, and only one person can fit through it at a time," Wally said. "You can't storm a castle one man at a time."

"Huh," Ariane said. "Well, thank you, Mr. Medieval Dictionary."

Wally stuck his tongue out at her.

They found the tunnel, which was fortunately missing the "locked and guarded" door it presumably had had once upon a time, right where he said it was. It would have been a surprise if they hadn't, since he'd already been through it once. Now they passed through a short tunnel and up a flight of worn stone stairs to the strip of land between the keep and the wall. Lights shone through four high-arched windows. "Mom said she'd be shooting in the Great Hall," Wally said. "Flish is bound to be in there with her. We can't grab her from there."

"Maybe we don't want to," Ariane said. "Maybe this is the chance you were hoping for, to talk to Flish, try to reason with her. With your mom there..."

"We can't talk about anything that's happened with Mom there," Wally said. "She'll think we're crazy. "

"But maybe that's better," Ariane said. "Maybe the only way you and Flish can figure anything out is if you have to deal with each other strictly on a brother-sister level, not on an Heirs-of-King-Arthur-pursuing-the-shards-of Excalibur level."

"And if it doesn't work?" Wally demanded.

"*Then* we grab her and teleport her somewhere out of the way," Ariane said. "Without Rex Major around, who's going to stop us?"

Wally looked unusually uncertain – for Wally. His face had become a bit more angular, a bit more grown-up, over the past few months, even as he'd somehow managed to overtake her in height. He'd lost most of his freckles over the winter, and his ears even seemed to fit his head better than they used to. But he still, more often than not, had the patented Wally-grin that she used to think was spectacularly ugly and now found spectacularly endearing. Though the grin did not appear this time – in fact, he was chewing his lip, which she didn't think she'd *ever* seen him do before.

"I don't know," he said, and she hadn't very often heard him say *that*, either.

"Wally, I know it's hard. You know I know it's hard – you were there when I found Mom at the Empress. Magical quests are easy; family is hard." She smiled a little. "And friendship. And love. And all that other stuff. It's all hard. But you can't avoid dealing with it just because it's hard. And you wouldn't want to if you could."

"'We choose to go to the moon in this decade and do the other things, not because they are easy, but because they are hard,'" Wally muttered.

Ariane blinked. "What?"

"Nothing. Ancient history." He took a deep breath. "All right. I'll talk to her." He hesitated. "Will you...will you come in with me? I'd like Mom to meet you."

Awww, Ariane thought, but she had to shake her head. "I don't think that's a good idea – not with Flish there. Not if there's going to be any chance of a reasonable discussion. Your mom doesn't even know I exist. Having to explain me would just complicate things."

Wally sighed. "I was afraid you'd be all reasonable and say that."

Ariane smiled a little. "I need to be outside anyway.

Both to keep watch in case Rex Major comes back, and in case we want to snatch Flish after all."

"Also very reasonable," Wally said. "Very mature. Must be a side effect of being an old woman of sixteen."

She stuck out her tongue at him.

He laughed a little. "All right." He looked up at the castle windows, then down and to the left. "This way."

He led Ariane up a bit of a slope to the main wall of the castle, then around one end of it, where he got down on his hands and knees and crawled forward through a screen of heather. At least, she guessed it was heather. Not that she'd ever seen heather before, but she figured any bush growing in Scotland was likely to be heather, wasn't it? She was sure Wally could have told her, but he was preoccupied.

On all fours on the wet ground, she looked out through the probably-heather over a kind of courtyard, the rain spattering on its cobblestones. No one was in sight, but a car and van were parked just at the foot of the surprisingly narrow steps that led up to the castle's main entrance. The stairs boasted steel handrails that were clearly far more modern than the building itself. Ariane wondered how much – or how little – of what she was looking at really dated back to the fourteenth century. What was that old joke, about the axe that had been in the family for a hundred years? *The handle's been replaced six times and the blade twice, but it's still the same axe!*

"I'll wait on the steps just outside the door," Ariane said.

Wally nodded. They walked to and up the steps together. Ariane stopped on the small porch at the top, beneath a wooden overhang that kept off some of the rain, and gave Wally a quick kiss. "For luck," she whispered into his ear.

He nodded, gave her a rather sickly version of the

Wally-grin, and turned and pushed open the heavy door. Made of oak and bound with rusty steel, *it* certainly looked as old as the castle was supposed to be. Ariane caught a brief glimpse of a vaulted hall as Wally turned and pushed the door closed again. Then he was gone.

Since she was alone and they'd seen Rex Major drive away, she ordered the rain that found its way under the overhang to stay away from her, sat down on the top step – dry despite the mist and drizzle – and settled in to keep watch.

CHAPTER FOUR

FAMILY REUNION

IT WAS AN ODD THING, when he thought about it, but Merlin had never before been to Scotland. In Arthur's day it had been wild and untamed lands populated by barbarians – and, as Rex Major, Merlin had been to enough functions in the south of England during his second lifetime on Earth to know there were plenty of Englishmen who thought it still was.

Yet here he was at last, in the twenty-first century.

He just wished he was there, because he had a lead on the location of the hilt of Excalibur, the last missing piece of the sword forged by the Lady of the Lake and given to Arthur back when his beloved sister and he had been on the same page – as they said in these modern times – about what they wanted to accomplish on Earth. Alas, his sister had withdrawn into Faerie with all the other...elves, he supposed some would call them, although he hated that term and the pointy-eared connotations of it. Still, to be sure, "elves" was better than "fairies." That had been when the Queen and her puppets, the Council of Clades, had decreed that Earth was not to be annexed after all, but abandoned, and that humans were to be left to their own devices, with the door between the worlds shut and sealed.

Merlin had refused to go, and had as a result been imprisoned – in an oak tree, of all things – for a millennium, through the treacherous wiles of the sorceress Viviane, who, he was furiously certain, had acted at his sister's command. But the Queen and the Lady had been unable to close the door between the worlds completely – Merlin's hand rose to the ruby stud in his right earlobe; a bad habit, he would admit, at least to himself – and so a trickle of magic had continued to seep through, slowly wearing away the walls of Viviane's enchantment like water wearing away stone, eventually freeing him.

He'd been working ever since to try to find the shards of Excalibur. That sword, reforged, could open wide the door between the worlds once more, giving him access to all his magical power of old, and a path to conquering Faerie and freeing it from the hidebound tyranny of the Queen and Council. To do so, of course, he first had to conquer Earth – or, at least, enough of it that he could build an earthly army with modern weapons to send through the door into Faerie.

He should have been able to do so unopposed. Who but himself could even know the sword existed in this world where Arthur himself had been reduced, not only to a mere legend – which would be bad enough – but to a fit subject for *musical theatre*, for God's sake?

But his blasted sister had known or suspected his prison would not last, and had put in place her own plans, gifting her power to a line of humans, her "heirs," before she abandoned Earth. And those humans had continued to pass her magic along unknowing, generation after generation, until, learning that Merlin had escaped, she chose to wake it.

Her first attempt had failed, the bearer of her magic refusing the powers she offered, but the daughter of that woman had accepted it – and had been a pain in Merlin's neck, and other parts of his anatomy, ever since.

Ariane Forsythe. A mere child whom he should have easily been able to crush or to cow, she had somehow managed to get two of the shards. Assisted by Wally Knight, his other candidate for most annoying teenager of the twenty-first century – a very broad category, for if there was one thing he detested about the current age it was its unhealthy obsessions with the young. Wisdom lay not with the young, but the old – as he should know, being the oldest man – if he used the term broadly – on Earth.

And yet, there had been a silver lining to Ariane's and Wally's interference, because it had turned out that Wally Knight was also heir to power – the power of King Arthur, for whom the sword had been specifically crafted. Unlike Ariane, who shared no genes with the Lady of the Lake – she was, after all, no more human than Merlin himself – Wally was an actual physical descendant of Arthur, through the king's rebellious son Mordred, and it was through his particular line, out of all the hundreds or thousands of family trees that by now shared a common ancestor in Arthur, that the magic had descended. Wally was attuned to the power of Excalibur as no other human could be...

...well, no other human but his own sister, Felicia.

When Merlin had begun his campaign to gather the shards of Excalibur, he'd had no idea an heir of Arthur could still be found. But the moment he'd realized what Wally was, he'd grasped the possibilities. He'd wanted Excalibur merely to open the door into Faerie. But Excalibur had other properties, too. Wielding it, Wally would be the most dangerous swordsman the world had seen since the original Arthur. Admittedly, that was of less importance now than it had been in Arthur's heyday – but it was only one indication of the sword's power. More importantly, an heir of Arthur, bearing Excalibur, would be a leader of men *par excellence*. They would fall at the sword-wielder's feet, begging to be led into battle. A new Arthur with Excalibur in hand would inspire fanatical loyalty in the forces, both human and Faerie, that Merlin intended to assemble to sweep away the Queen and Council of Clades like tumbleweeds in a prairie wind.

Wally had betrayed him, returning to Ariane's side – *teen hormones*, he thought in disgust – but Felicia was different. She hated Ariane, and was almost as furious with her brother as Merlin was with his sister. More, she wanted power. True, she'd always thought of it in terms of popularity and fame and wealth, but the desire was the same, and Merlin could work with it – *had* worked with it. Felicia would do what he needed done, and after all, this wasn't post-Roman Britain anymore. Rex Major was a modern-day businessman and diversity was all the rage. Who better to lead his new armies than a woman?

With Felicia's help, he'd retrieved the fourth shard from its hiding place in a cave in the Caribbean. She'd been a little squeamish about the way he'd dealt with her brother, who had grabbed the shard from Felicia and almost escaped with it. But he'd calmed her down by convincing her that he'd sent help for Wally after they'd left him unconscious on the side of a hill, knocked out by the blast of a lightning bolt Merlin had called down just behind him.

Of course, he'd sent no such help. If Wally had died, it would have made things easier all around, and possibly broken Ariane's spirit, but until Felicia was thoroughly under his thumb, he needed to make a few concessions to her childish sensibilities.

He thought he'd made great progress on the getting-her-under-his-thumb front over the five months since. She'd settled very contentedly into her new life with him in Toronto – not too surprising, since it was exactly the kind of lifestyle she'd always aspired to. He introduced her everywhere they went as his niece. Gallery openings, operas, dinners, charity balls – she'd eaten it up. He wondered if she were aware that it was widely rumoured she wasn't really his niece at all, but something else entirely.

Which was true, of course, but not at all in the way the gossipers thought.

Meanwhile, he'd been waiting…and waiting…and *waiting* for a hint as to the location of the final piece of the sword – the hilt. The two shards he had should have called to it – but they wouldn't, not while the infuriating Ariane had two of her own. Always before, he'd located a shard when some piece of technology infiltrated by the web of magic he had spun through the Internet drew close to it. But wherever the hilt was, no one seemed to be coming anywhere near it with an active smartphone.

He'd had a team of researchers trace Ariane's family back as far as they could, to see if there might be some hint in that history as to where the hilt might be hidden, to no avail.

But then, during one of his regular conversations with Jessica Knight, née MacPhaiden, Wally and Felicia's mother – whom he called regularly, as he did her estranged husband, to reinforce the magical Commands that kept them from wondering just what they were doing allowing their eighteen-year-old daughter to live with a much older man in a luxury penthouse in Toronto – she'd told him about her exciting new film project, for which she was currently raising funding. It was to be a personal odyssey in search of her family's roots in the British Isles, and it had suddenly occurred to him that maybe he'd been barking up the wrong family tree; that the hint as to the whereabouts of the hilt of Excalibur might lie, not with the heirs of the Lady, but with the heirs of Arthur.

Jessica had told him that she was still short of funds, and he'd promised not only to fund the project fully, but also to bring Felicia to the British Isles so she and her mother could learn about their family history together. Jessica had been ecstatic. Merlin thought the project was unlikely to really pay off in a solid lead as to the whereabouts of the hilt of Excalibur, but the truth was – though he would never have admitted it to anyone – he was getting more than a little desperate. Months had gone by, and nothing. What if the hilt was simply...gone? It had been more than a thousand years since the shards of Excalibur had been scattered, after all.

He *thought* that was impossible. He thought magic would work its way through events to protect the sword, just as it had clearly worked its way through history to bring the heir of the Lady's power and the heirs of Arthur's to Regina at the same time, to accept the Lady's quest to find the shards before Merlin did – but a thousand years was a very long time, especially on Earth in the past few centuries, where things had changed so fast and so much. Unlike in Faerie, where nothing ever changed, and never would unless Merlin changed it.

So here they were, at a dime-a-dozen castle near one of the drabbest and most unremarkable villages Merlin had ever seen anywhere (and considering the general state of villages in Arthur's day, that was saying something). Jessica had set up shop in the Great Hall – if you could call it that; compared to the Great Hall of Camelot it was a broom closet – and was getting ready to record a segment whose script she'd already shown to Major – all about how this castle had been stolen from its original builders by her ancestors in a bloody massacre at a wedding, and how it was from here her great-great-great-great-something or other had blah-blah-blah and...

None of it had anything to do with Arthur, and so Merlin had excused himself from the set – politely; he could *act* the part of a gentlemen to perfection – claiming he needed to run down to the town on business. Which was true enough – the village had Wi-Fi, and the castle did not, or at least none he could access.

But not far from the castle, as he drove along the rain-swept road, he suddenly sensed power – a power he recognized instantly.

Ariane Forsythe, heir to the Lady of the Lake, was near. *Very* near. And that could mean only one thing.

Far from acting on a long shot or embarking on a wild-goose chase, they'd come to exactly the right place at the right time. If Ariane was here, then either the hilt was here, or some hint of its whereabouts could be found here.

He didn't stop at once – he didn't want to spook his quarry. Instead, he carried on a couple of kilometres farther, until a bend in the road took him out of sight of the castle. Then he pulled the Jaguar over to the side of the road, got out, and hiked back through the rain until he could see the fortified hill again through the mist – which unfortunately had grown so thick he had to trudge almost back to the very spot where he had sensed Ariane's power, not far from a small loch.

He squinted up at the castle's dim bulk, and saw them, just for an instant – two small figures at the foot of the wall. Ariane and Wally, searching for the hilt. They vanished, and he turned and jogged back to his car. Ignoring his wet feet and sopping suit, he opened the trunk – the boot, they called it over here – and brought out a small black case he'd taken to carrying with him everywhere, hoping he'd have a chance to use it. It looked as if he'd get his wish at last, and the thought made him grin in fierce anticipation.

He put the case down on the black leather of the passenger seat, then eased the Jag around and drove back up the hill to Castle MacPhaiden.

In all of the adventures he'd had thus far in the quest for the shards of Excalibur, Wally's heart had never raced the way it raced as he climbed the steps of the castle to meet his mother.

She's not as scary as Emeka, Major's henchman I clobbered with a tree branch outside the YMCA in Gravenhurst...or Major himself...or being dissolved into water or clouds and magically transported halfway around the world, he reminded himself.

To which himself replied, *Wanna bet?*

Beyond the thick wooden door lay a surprisingly small entrance hall – well, surprisingly small if you thought of the old castle as a modern house, but maybe not if you thought of it as a place designed to be easily defended. At the end of a hall lit by a wheel-shaped chandelier of black iron and furnished with an old, scarred table and two uncomfortable-looking chairs carved from dark wood along the right wall, the corridor turned sharply left beneath a faded red tapestry. Wally went to the corner, only to find yet another hallway, this one even narrower and not furnished at all. There was a closed door on his left, and another closed door directly ahead, where the corridor bent to the right.

Now he heard voices coming from around that corner. He walked down to it, his sopping-wet runners silent on the worn stones of the floor, water dripping from his hair down the back of his neck, and found that the corridor continued only a short distance farther. At its end, a surprisingly small suit of armour – Wally didn't think he could have fit into it – stood guard next to an arch that opened to the left. Light flooded through that arch, the unnaturally bright illumination of movie lighting.

Wally went to the archway, and took a cautious peek

around the corner into the Great Hall.

The chamber was reasonably impressive, if perhaps not all that "great;" he figured it was about twenty-five metres long and maybe ten metres wide. Set in the left wall he could see an enormous fireplace, big enough to stand up in. In the right wall were the four tall windows he had seen from outside, filled with tiny diamond-shaped panes of glass.

Two doors opened off the far end of the Great Hall, both closed; the one on the right looked like a swinging door, which definitely wasn't original equipment. Between the doors rose a dais, three steps up from the floor, that might once have held a throne. Another ancient, fading tapestry, this one depicting warriors battling each other in front of forested hills, covered the wall behind the dais. It was in front of that tapestry that his mom had set up her lights and cameras, the crew running around doing the usual preparations that always looked aimless to Wally even though he knew there must be some sort of method to it. His mom sat on the top step of the dais watching the two men and the woman work.

Beside her sat Flish.

Wally stepped back from the arch. With the camera lights shining in their eyes he didn't think they could see him in the shadows, and it gave him a chance to study them both.

The Rex Major lifestyle clearly agreed with Flish, who, just like in the picture they'd seen in Weyburn, looked older than her eighteen years – and *way* overdressed, in a short black dress and high heels. A necklace glittered in the lights; probably not diamond, he thought, but then again, maybe it was.

Mom had her hand on Felicia's knee and was talking to her earnestly. Wally wondered what they were talking about.

Well, one way to find out.

He took a deep breath and a hard swallow, then stepped through the archway and started walking the length of the Great Hall toward his mother and sister.

Between the lights and their conversation they didn't notice him right away; in fact, the cinematographer saw him first. "Hey!" the man said. "You're not supposed to –" Then his eyes widened. "Whoa! Wally, is that you?"

"Hi, Jim," Wally said.

Everyone stopped what they were doing and stared at Wally, who kept walking, across a floor that seemed to somehow extend further with every step so that the dais and his mother and sister never seemed to get any closer. At first they just stared at him, too, both of them. Then his mom rose wavering to her feet. "Wally?" she choked out.

Flish just sat like a statue, glaring at him.

He hadn't planned what he was going to say, he realized as he opened his mouth, but then he heard himself say, "Happy Mother's Day," and suddenly Mom was running toward him, and the distance between them he'd seemed unable to close evapourated in an instant. She grabbed him in a fierce hug and pulled him close, and suddenly all the years and all the problems evapourated too, and Wally was a small boy again and his mom was just Mom, and as long as she was hugging him, nothing could be wrong with the world.

The moment couldn't last, and it didn't last, but Wally wouldn't have traded it for all the money – or all the magical swords – in the world.

It was Flish who ruined it, of course, Flish who rose to her feet and stalked toward both of them on her high heels like a long-legged shore bird looking for something small and slimy to stab with its beak. "You've got some nerve, showing up here!" she said, her voice colder than the water still dripping from Wally's hair.

"Felicia!" Mom cried. "Aren't you glad to see your brother?"

"After the way he's treated you and Dad?" Flish shot back. "And me? Running away from Rex Major, after everything Rex did for him?"

So he's "Rex" now, Wally noted.

"Stealing money and flying to New Zealand?" Flish raged on. "Disappearing? You thought he was dead, and he never even called to say he was safe until long afterward. He still hasn't called you. He only called Dad. Some brother. Some *son*."

"Felicia!" Mom snapped, and this time there was real anger in her voice. She looked around at the crew. "All of you, get out of here," she ordered. "Take an early lunch. My kids and I clearly need to talk."

The three crewmembers, who had been watching wide-eyed, exchanged guilty glances and then hurried out of the Great Hall, although not in the direction of the main entrance. Instead, they exited through the swinging door to the right of the dais. Wally glimpsed a modern kitchen, all stainless steel and white tile, as they passed through.

Mom turned back to Felicia. "Felicia, stop this. It's been a difficult time for all of us. For the whole family. We've all had trouble dealing with it. At least Wally *did* finally let your father know he was still alive." But Wally heard the uncertainty in Mom's voice as she spoke to her daughter, and saw it in her eyes as she turned around again. "But...how did you get *here*, Wally?"

"I came with a friend," Wally said. "Mom, I'm all right, really. And I'm sorry I didn't call, but I didn't want Rex Major to know where I was." He gave Flish a hard stare. "He's not our friend, Mom. You should get Felicia away from him. He's not a nice man."

Let her interpret that however she wants, he thought savagely. *In fact, the sleazier the better.*

"He's lying, Mom," Flish snapped back. "Rex Major has never been anything other than a perfect gentlemen to me. And he's giving me such wonderful opportunities. Wally's just jealous he threw that all away. And I'm not surprised he doesn't want Rex to know where he is, considering how much money he stole from him."

"Is that true, Wally?" Mom said.

Wally wanted to deny it, but he couldn't without lying, and he didn't want to lie to his mom – well, not any more than he could help, anyway. "I only took what I needed to get away from him, Mom. And I *had* to get away from him, to save myself."

"Save yourself from what?" Flish said scornfully. She looked at Mom. "You want to know how he got here? He got here with the money he stole from Rex. *Thousands of dollars*, Mom." She rounded on Wally again. "Bet you didn't expect to see *me* here, did you?"

Anger, hot as a forest fire, roared up in Wally, and suddenly he didn't care if Mom thought they were crazy, didn't care *what* she thought. He knew the sword was feeding the flames of his fury, the two shards Ariane carried reaching out to him through the stone of the castle walls, but he didn't need the sword to make him angry with Felicia, who had once been his best friend and hero and had chosen – *her* choice, not his – to transform herself into his enemy.

"And I'll bet you didn't expect to see me here either, did you?" he snarled. "Since you happily went off with Rex Major and left me for dead on Cacibajagua!"

"I did not!" Flish said furiously. "I made Rex Major send men for you, to make sure you were all right."

"Liar," Wally said. "No one came. If Ariane hadn't found me, I probably would have drowned face down in the rain on that path."

"What are you two talking about?" Mom cried.

"Cacibajagua? Wally, you almost *died?* And who is Ariane?"

Flish took no notice. "That bitchy girlfriend of yours broke my leg. She might have killed me. And you didn't care."

"Of course I cared! What do you think drove me to Rex Major in the first place?"

That brought Flish up short. She blinked. "What?"

"I joined Major – for a while – because I didn't like what the shards were doing to Ariane," Wally snarled, still furious. "What they made her do to *you*. But then I found out what Major was really like. He held Ariane's Aunt Phyllis hostage. He threatened to kill Ariane's mom. He would have let me die on that hillside. You're *blind*, Felicia. Your hatred of Ariane is keeping you from seeing what Major is really like." He glared at her. "Or maybe it's the glitter from that necklace that's blinding you. You're so in love with yourself and Rex Major's money you don't care what he's done or plans to do. You don't care about anyone but yourself!"

He knew at once he'd gone too far. Flish's eyes narrowed again and the moment of doubt, of openness, vanished as though it had never been.

She opened her mouth to retort, but Mom cut her off. "Stop it, you two! Sit down!" She pointed to the dais. Wally hesitated, still glaring at Flish. "Sit down!" Mom said again, even more sharply, and both of them responded to the parental version of Merlin's Voice of Command by walking stiffly to the dais and sitting just as stiffly on either side of Mom.

"Someone tell me what's going on," Mom demanded. "Shards? Threats? Hostages?"

Wally shook his head. "I can't," he said stubbornly.

Flish didn't speak at all, just sat with her lips pressed into a tight white line.

Mom looked from one to the other. "Never mind, then. Tell me later. What matters is family. You two are *family*. We can work this out." She put a hand on Wally's knee, and her voice softened. "I know it's been hard, Wally." She glanced at her daughter, and put her other hand on the girl's knee. "Felicia." She looked down, away from either of them. "Since your father..." Her voice died away.

"Took up with a blonde bimbo?" Flish offered harshly. "Dumped you for a younger woman? Started fu –"

Mom's head jerked up. "That's enough, Felicia!" She took a deep breath. "Yes. Since all of that. I didn't...I know work has kept me away a lot these last few years, more than it should have, maybe, but I never thought he'd..." She shook her head. "I didn't know how to cope. I couldn't come home. I couldn't bear...I couldn't bear to see him, and I couldn't bear to see either one of you, because I felt like I'd betrayed you – *we'd* betrayed you, failed you. I didn't know how to talk to you about what had happened. I barely even knew how to think about it. I kept playing with possibilities in my mind, like it was a movie scene I had to direct, but I could never get the script or my own performance to come out right. And I couldn't begin to imagine how you might react. So I just...hid. Ran away."

She blinked away tears, and smiled, a little wetly, at Flish. "I was so happy when Rex Major said he'd fund this project, not just because I needed the funding, but because I hoped that maybe it meant I would see you more. And here you are."

She turned that smile, teary-eyed and tentative but genuine, on Wally, and the sight of her tears melted away a lot of his anger, dousing the flame of his rage in a flood of love and regret. "But to see you here, too...to have both of my children together on Mother's Day...I never thought..." Her hands squeezed their knees. "Don't fight, children. Please. Can't we just...enjoy being together, as a family? Like we used to? We could go down to the village, sightsee, get something to eat…"

Wally looked at Flish. For a moment they weren't enemies, weren't rivals on opposite sides of a quest to find the shards of Excalibur. They were just brother and sister, and Wally discovered, almost to his surprise, that he really wanted that moment to last, as much as he had wanted the moment when his mom hugged him to last.

But he still needed to know if what his mom was working on might point them – or Rex Major – to the hilt of Excalibur. And changing the subject right now seemed like the best way to keep the fragile peace among them anyway. "Mom…what is this project you're working on anyway? Is it a movie?"

"Not exactly," Mom said. "It's…well, it's a personal odyssey. A journey of discovery. Our family's history is… unusual. Your father's family, the Knights, and my family, the MacPhaidens, have deep roots in the British Isles. Deep roots, and tangled ones, too."

Wally blinked. "What does that mean?"

Mom smiled at him, clearly pleased he was taking an interest. "It's the strangest thing. Down through the centuries, the two families keep intermarrying. Generation after generation, a Knight would marry a MacPhaiden. Sometimes the woman was a Knight, sometimes she was a MacPhaiden, like me. Sometimes the pattern skipped a couple of generations…but before you knew it, the Knights and MacPhaidens found each other again.

"I don't know if you know this, but your great-great-grandmother on your father's side was actually a MacPhaiden, related to me. So your Great-Grandfather Knight was a mixture of the Knights and the MacPhaidens, just like you two are."

"That's…interesting," Wally said, but his mind was racing. *This magic business is even weirder than I thought.*

Somehow the Lady's magic, instilled in Excalibur, had wound its way through the lives of his ancestors, generation after generation, binding the Knights and MacPhaidens together, ensuring that the thread of magic originating in King Arthur was passed along, that it would appear the moment it was needed, when at last Excalibur was to be reforged.

There was a legend, he remembered, that King Arthur had not died, but had simply been spirited away, to reappear and claim the throne of Britain again when the island nation was in its greatest hour of need. Maybe there was something to that, although Wally and Felicia Knight popping up in Regina, Saskatchewan, perhaps didn't *quite* fit the bill.

Mom could never guess the Arthurian connection, because she couldn't possibly trace the family back that far. There simply were no records of the time of the historical King Arthur, which was why there was serious doubt that he *was* historical.

For a moment he was tempted to tell her…but just as she had been unable to picture a scenario in which she successfully talked to her children about the breakup of their parents' marriage, he was incapable of coming up with a scenario in which he claimed to be the heir to King Arthur on a quest to reforge Excalibur, the quest given to him by the Lady of the Lake – whose own heir also happened to be his girlfriend – without his mother figuring he was crazy or on drugs, or both.

The part about me having a girlfriend might be the most unbelievable of all.

"I've always wanted to visit the British Isles and trace our family history as far back as I can," Mom said. "Castle MacPhaiden here seemed like a good place to start, even if the way it came into the family was rather…unsavoury."

"This whole MacPhaiden/Knight thing sounds pretty unbelievable," Wally said. "All that intermarrying... wouldn't someone have noticed before now?"

"It's not as easy to tease out of the records as you might think," Mom said. "The MacPhaidens and Knights seem to have gone out of their way to keep a low profile for...well, for centuries. Some records even look like they were altered by someone trying to hide the connection. I might not have twigged to it at all if not for the papers left by your Great-Grandfather Knight – you remember, he immigrated to Cannington Manor, told your Grandma Knight when she wrote that book of hers a story about fleeing to Canada with a great treasure." She grinned at Wally. "You've always liked fantasy stories, so you'll like this. My theory is your Great-Grandpa believed the two families stayed so close down through the centuries because they were nothing less than the sacred keepers of the Holy Grail, and that he honestly believed that the Grail was the 'treasure' he'd brought with him. And apparently promptly lost. Certainly your Grandma never saw it."

"Great-Grandpa Knight was probably just crazy," Felicia put in. She sat with her arms folded across her expensive necklace, glowering at Wally. "It runs in the family."

But Wally hardly noticed the jibe. His mind was racing even faster than his heart had been when he'd first come into the Great Hall.

How could he have forgotten Great-Grandpa Knight and his mysterious "treasure?" He'd even told Ariane and Aunt Phyllis about it, way back in the fall when all this had started, one night when he'd gone to their house for dinner. He remembered describing Great-Grandpa's time as one of the Cannington Manor "bachelors," the single men with no inheritance or place in their families, sent out west to make their way in the world. Supposedly they had come to Cannington Manor to learn to farm, but most of them seemed to have come to party.

He'd even mentioned Great-Grandpa's claim of having travelled to Canada with a treasure, and his conviction he dared not return to Great Britain because it wouldn't be safe.

It had just been a story, a way to make conversation. Like Flish, he'd always figured maybe Great-Grandpa Knight was a little crazy, a little paranoid.

But what if he hadn't been?

What if he really *had* had a treasure? And what if it really *was* an ancient artifact – but not the one his mother was thinking of? Not the Holy Grail, but the final piece of the sword Excalibur, the hilt, given into the safekeeping of Arthur's descendants for more than a millennium, the magic within it constantly weaving around its guardians, always keeping the Knights and MacPhaidens close.

The thought boggled his mind, and maybe it was just wishful thinking.

But what if it wasn't?

He didn't want Felicia following his train of thought – though it might already be too late. What if Rex Major had been driving off as they approached precisely because he had already heard Wally's mom say something that had sent him racing back to Canada to look for the hilt?

He forced a laugh and studiously avoided looking at Flish. "I like fantasy stories, Mom, but get real. There's no such thing as the Holy Grail."

His mom shrugged. "Of course not. But it'll be a great angle to hang the film on. The Holy Grail is an evergreen. If I can just tie the family to the Knights Templar I'll really have something."

"So what are you shooting here?" Wally said, looking around the Great Hall.

"Just the introduction," Mom said. "A description of the bloody wedding feast at which this castle changed hands in 1478."

"Who killed who?"

"Whom," Mom corrected. "It was the MacPhaidens, I'm afraid. The wedding, which was supposed to bury the hatchet between them and the clan that had built the castle, was really just a ruse to get them inside the keep. Two years later the daughter they used as bait married someone else in this very hall." She shuddered. "Cold-blooded lot, our ancestors."

"Let me guess," Wally said. "The daughter went on to marry an ancestor of the Knights."

His mom nodded. "Weird, huh?"

"Weird," Flish muttered. "Like this whole conversation." She got to her feet. "I can't take this anymore. It's not just the *history* of this family that's weird. The whole *family* is weird." She jabbed a red-painted fingernail at Wally. "Rex Major will be back soon. If you know what's good for you, you won't be here when he comes back. Remember what happened last time you crossed him. Get out of his way, get away from that bitchfriend of yours, and you won't get hurt again. And that's the last thing I have to say to you." She withdrew the accusing finger. "Goodbye, Mom. Maybe I'll see you later...but don't count on it."

She stalked down the dais steps and headed toward the archway leading to the main entrance, high heels clicking on the stone floor. Mom leaped up. "Flish!" she cried. "Come back!"

"I'll get her," Wally said hastily. He had to be with Flish when she met Ariane on the steps. "I'll..." *be back in a minute,* he intended to say, but again, he didn't want to lie to his mother, and he didn't know if that was true. Most likely, it wasn't. He let the sentence drop into silence and ran after Flish.

"Flish, wait!" he called as she reached the archway. Somewhat to his surprise, she actually did, turning to face him as he ran up to her.

"I told you, I'm done talking to you," she snapped.

"But we haven't really talked, have we?" Wally said, trying to sound reasonable. "We couldn't, with Mom there. Flish, I –"

"I think we've talked enough," Flish snarled, and spun and headed down the hallway toward the main entrance.

Wally hurried after her. When she emerged from the castle door, and Ariane grabbed her, he wanted to be close enough to go with them. Otherwise he'd have to wait for Ariane to come back for him, and Rex Major might return in the interim. And Flish had gotten one thing right – he did *not* want to be there when Rex Major came back. Not out of fear for his own safety – well, not *just* out of that fear – but because the last thing he wanted was for Rex Major to start thinking about Jessica Knight as a hostage. Or to start thinking about the family history, and Great-Grandpa Knight's mysterious treasure.

Flish disappeared into the main entrance hall. Wally quickened his steps, and rounded the final corner just in time to see her open the main door. Thick fog seemed to have descended on the castle – he couldn't see a thing outside except a grey mist…

Which suddenly vanished, revealing Ariane.

Flish stopped dead, but Wally broke into a run.

CHAPTER FIVE

FADING INTO DARKNESS

"Keeping watch on the castle steps" would probably have sounded pretty exciting in a book, but in real life, as Ariane quickly discovered, it offered roughly as many thrills as watching paint dry.

Or not dry, considering how hard it was raining.

At least I'll have plenty of water to work with if Rex Major comes back.

Not that she thought that was likely. He had probably dropped Flish off to watch whatever her mom was doing in the castle while he went off to the village, or even farther – Ariane had only the vaguest idea of distances in Scotland, but she doubted it was very far to anywhere compared to what she was used to in Saskatchewan – to attend to business.

Ariane both wished she had been inside the Great Hall to see what had happened when Wally met his mother and confronted Flish, and was very happy she *hadn't* been. She'd never met Wally's mother – or his father, for that matter, although she'd at least seen him from a distance in Victoria when she'd opened up the Empress Hotel's fire sprinklers over his head so he wouldn't spot Wally. But all she knew about Jessica Knight was that she made movies and she hadn't been around for months.

Oh, and that uncomfortable business about how his father had moved out to be with a younger woman.

She sighed. *Families are hard*, she thought again. *Harder than magical quests.*

She'd never known her own father. He'd also moved out, whether to be with another woman or just to get away from his impending fatherhood, she didn't know – but at least he'd had the decency, from her point of view, to do so before she was born. She didn't know who he was, and her mom had never told her. Maybe she'd ask sometime, but not now – not when they were still trying to piece back together something approaching a good relationship.

She thought she'd done pretty well, considering her mom had abandoned her to foster homes and pretended she didn't know who Ariane was, after the Lady of the Lake had approached her and asked her to take the power Ariane had eventually claimed. Mom had thought she was doing it for Ariane's good, and Ariane understood that, and could even appreciate it...

...but it didn't change the fact that Mom hadn't been around as Ariane turned into a teenager, right when she could have used a mom the most.

She still felt anger every time she thought of it, anger she tried hard to control, although the power of the shards of Excalibur she now carried with her all the time made anger much, much harder to manage than it used to be. And she'd never been all that great at anger management even *before* the shards hacked their way into her life.

She knew Wally, too, felt the power of the shards, differently in some ways, but very much the same in others. And one way in which the power was the same for both of them was the anger, the desire to strike out at enemies, real or imagined, to take revenge for past wrongs. She hoped he didn't blow up at his mom. *He must feel almost as abandoned as I did. And his mom doesn't even have my mom's trying-to-protect-you-from-a-millennium-old-magical-feud excuse.*

There was no way she could hear anything through the old castle's thick stone walls, but that didn't stop her from straining her ears.

The rain strengthened, and the wind with it, so that the water slashed almost horizontally across the courtyard, and the tops of the trees visible above the outbuildings on the far side of the courtyard thrashed frenetically. Beyond that, the treeless, heather-covered slope of the hill behind the castle rose sharply up until it disappeared into mist; the clouds had come down the hillside along with the rain, and Ariane was glad now she hadn't had to try the trick-Merlin-into-thinking-she'd-found-the-hilt ruse she'd come up with earlier. She would have been invisible if she'd gone up there, and wouldn't be able to see what was happening down here in the castle courtyard, either.

She exerted a little more of her power to keep the water another few inches away from her body. She couldn't do anything about the temperature, though, and she was dressed for May in Saskatchewan – which *could* be cool, but hadn't been – not for Mother's Day in Scotland. And, of course, since they didn't have regular access to the Internet, they hadn't even been able to check the forecast before they came.

Minutes ticked by. Just to amuse herself, she not only ordered the water not to touch her, she ordered it to swirl around her and break up into smaller and smaller droplets until she sat inside her own personal cloud, cut off from the outside world. *Or maybe the outside world is cut off from me*, she thought, and grinned. *What's that old joke about how the English view the world? "Fog in the Channel, Continent cut off?"*

She grinned wider.

A loud clank startled her – the latch on the castle door! She said a bad word and let the fog drop...

...only to find herself staring straight at a black Jaguar pulling into the courtyard, Rex Major at the wheel, while at the same instant, Felicia stormed through the now-open door.

Wally's sister stopped dead. "You!"

Wally himself came pounding down the hallway behind her. "Hold her!" Ariane shouted to him, and grabbed Flish's wrist while Wally wrapped his arms her from behind.

"Let go of me!" Flish screamed. Ariane ignored her and reached for her magic, intending to hurl all three of them into the clouds and away from Rex Major, who was just getting out of the Jaguar, holding something in his right hand...*is that a pistol?*

But for the first time since she'd said "Yes" to the Lady, the magic failed her. It rebounded from Flish, who remained as firmly in place as if she were a Flish-shaped statue Ariane had tried to pick up from the ground with her ordinary physical strength. She could feel the power flowing to her from the shards, *both* shards, with Wally *and* Flish so close, but Flish, impervious, twisted free and stumbled backward a couple of steps. A savage grin spread across her face. "I don't know what you're trying to do, but it's not going to work, is it?" she crowed. "I can *feel* it. You can't use your magic on me!"

Wally gaped at Flish, then at Ariane. "What...?"

"I don't know!" Ariane cried. She held out her hand. "Quick, we've got to get out of here. Rex Major..."

Wally glanced past her at Major. His eyes jerked wide and his face paled. He reached out to Ariane...

...and just as their hands met, Major raised the pistol-thing in his right hand. There was no flash of light, no crack of a gunshot, but something stung Ariane in the side of the neck, a sharp, piercing pain, and even as she dissolved into the clouds, she felt her consciousness swirling sickly away.

◄◄ ►►

Merlin swore. He knew he'd hit the blasted brat, but she'd managed to get away all the same.

Or had she? He stared at the place from which she and Wally had disappeared, eyes narrowed. If the tranquilizer dart had had any time at all to take effect, just how much in control of her power had she been as she dissolved into the storm?

He turned and tossed the air pistol back onto the seat of the Jaguar as Felicia dashed across the courtyard toward him. Well, as much of a dash as she could manage in her ridiculous high heels. It was really more of a teeter-tottering stagger. "Did you see that?" she cried. She'd been doing less of the surly teen act in recent months, as she'd settled into the kind of life Major's wealth and connections could provide, but even so, he'd rarely seen her face as alight with excitement as it was at that moment. "She tried to drag me away with her and she couldn't! She couldn't!" Felicia spun around in the rain, arms outstretched. "I could feel it!" she exulted. "I could feel her magic sliding right off of me like I had a non-stick coating! She'll never be able to use it against me again!"

"She may not be able to use it against anyone ever again," Merlin said.

Felicia stopped spinning and stared at him. "What?"

She was ridiculously overdressed, in her little black dress and high heels, and she looked rather pathetic with her red hair plastered to her skull by the rain, but she didn't seem to notice, still caught up in the excitement of her unexpected resistance to the Lady's power. Merlin wasn't surprised by that resistance, of course – Felicia, like Wally, was heir to the power of King Arthur, and Arthur had been given control of the sword by the Lady when she'd first forged it. Felicia had not *wanted* the sword to help transport her away from the castle, and so the sword had refused to allow its power to be used that way. Wally could have stopped Ariane transporting him, too, anytime he wanted, but of course Wally *wanted* to travel with Ariane. It was as simple as that.

The other question, though... "I hit her with a tran-quilizer dart just before she disappeared," he said. "Ever since my men almost managed to capture her in Graven-hurst using chloroform, I've realized that I can stop her using her power if I can knock her out before she can draw on it."

"But you were too late," Felicia said. "She got away."

"She disappeared into the clouds," Merlin corrected. "The question is – will she ever reappear?"

Felicia's eyebrows knit together. "What?"

"Magic is dangerous," Merlin said. "Not just to those against whom it is used as a weapon, but for those who wield it. When my power is at its full, I can draw demons to me from the hellish realm where they reside – I still had one I summoned before my imprisonment and had kept on retainer, you might say, that I sent to trouble Ariane's dreams when this whole business started – but I have rarely done it. For all my skill, there is a not-negligible risk that I could lose control of the demon, and a demon who breaks free from a sorcerer controlling it always, *always* kills the sorcerer. I can call down lightning, as you saw on Cacibajagua Island, but were my concentration to slip, I could easily call it down on myself, and the fact I was the one who called it would no more protect me from the consequences than the fact a race car driver *was* in complete control of his car protects him from the consequences when he *loses* control. So, if Ariane lost control of her magic, well…" Merlin shrugged, "that might be the last we see of her."

"But she had the shards with her," Felicia said. Then her eyes widened and her face, which was pale to begin with – typical of redheads – paled even further, so she looked like the flame-haired ghost of the long-dead mother-of-the-groom who was said to haunt the halls of Castle MacPhaiden. "She had *Wally* with her."

Careful, Merlin thought; he'd again just brushed up against that soft spot she still had for her little brother. Fortunately, once the sword was complete and she took it in hand, he was confident its single-minded bloodthirstiness would wipe out this final annoying hangover of her previous life, and she'd never again give her family a second thought. He imagined the same would happen to Wally, if he ever wielded Excalibur. *I wonder if Ariane told him that?* he thought. *No, probably not. I doubt she knows. There's so much she doesn't know, since she's had no contact with the Lady since this all started – thanks to my forcing my sister completely out of the world that day she popped up in Wascana Lake.*

"He'll just reappear somewhere, lost, maybe, but safe and sound," Merlin lied. In fact, he thought it certain that if Ariane lost her way in the clouds and dispersed to the four corners of the world as nothing more than a mist and a memory, Wally would meet exactly the same fate. "Just like the shards. They'll simply drop from the sky, or to the bottom of some stream or lake."

"But if they do, how will you find them?" Felicia said, and he noted with satisfaction she seemed to have accepted his comforting falsehood about her brother's possible fate.

I can't Command her, but she's only a teenage girl. I'll buy her another dress or another pretty necklace when we get back to Toronto and she'll never think about her brother again.

"If they are freed from the Lady's influence because Ariane is...no more, I'll be able to sense them through the two shards I have," he said out loud, and this time he was telling the truth. "And with you to help me draw on the shards' magic, I can retrieve them from anywhere. Even the bottom of the ocean, if it comes to that."

Which it very well might, if Wally and Ariane were over the ocean, heading for Saskatchewan, when Ariane... slipped away.

He smiled. The image pleased him.

"When will you know?" Felicia said. She *wasn't* smiling, which surprised him. He knew she hated Ariane. *Surely she will be glad when Ariane is dead?*

If he'd had his own shards of Excalibur with him, she would have had no doubts at all – he was certain of it. The sword loved the imagined deaths of enemies. It loved their actual deaths even more, and that attitude would have bled into Felicia. But he didn't like to carry the shards around with him, not when Ariane and Wally could pop up at any time – as they had here, of all places. His two pieces of Excalibur were locked in a very secure and very, very *dry* safe in a Toronto bank building.

"Not until I can have hold of my own shards," he said. "Which suddenly seems a very important thing to arrange. So say goodbye to your mother. We're driving straight to Inverness and flying back to Toronto."

Felicia turned and looked back through the rain at the castle. "I said what I wanted to say to her," she said. "And that included goodbye. Let's get out of here."

Excellent, Major thought. *Already, the sword begins to*

cut through the ties of family. "I'll contact your mother later and let her know what we're doing," he said smoothly. "And ask her how the filming is coming along."

"Whatever," Felicia said. She sounded like her old surly self, but for once Major approved. She got into the passenger side of the Jaguar. Major crossed in front of the car and got in on the driver's side.

He'd never turned off the engine; he shifted into drive and headed away from Castle MacPhaiden. Whatever secrets of family history it might conceal now held far less interest for him. If Ariane were truly out of the way – and he dared to allow himself to hope that that was the most likely outcome of what had just happened – then centuries-old hints of the hilt's whereabouts, if they even existed, no longer mattered.

He would take his own two shards of Excalibur in hand, and without the power of his sister to interfere, he would soon enough have the whole sword.

And then this world, and his own, would see what *real* power was.

He smiled, and accelerated into the rain.

◄◄ ►►

Something's wrong! Wally thought.

Travelling with Ariane was always terrifying, like being trapped in a dream, one of those dreams where you can't see anything clearly but you know something horrible is lurking just out of sight, ready to grab you, and you wake up with your heart racing, drenched with sweat.

But this…this was different.

Always before, when they entered cloud or stream or lake, he had felt that Ariane was still with him, disembodied though they both were. He could feel her as surely as if he stood next to her, holding his hand. Indeed, that was the way he usually interpreted it, as her hand somehow still being solid in the swirling watery darkness. He could always feel her fingers clutching his, a firm anchor ensuring he didn't go whirling away into the chaos and vanish forever.

But not this time...

This time, he could feel those fingers slipping away. Her grasp felt loose, her "hand" insubstantial and flimsy, and growing more so. And he could feel the chaos closing in on them both, could feel bits of himself dissolving, darkness nibbling at the edges of his consciousness. For the first time in all the journeys they'd made together, he didn't feel as if Ariane were in control. In truth, he didn't feel as if she was there at all. It was if she were unconscious, or almost so...

Unconscious.

He remembered Rex Major raising his right hand, something in it that looked frighteningly like a pistol. There hadn't been a gunshot, but there had been a flicker of something, a silver streak through the rain.

He's tranquilized her! Wally thought, and real panic roared up in him. *She's fading, and I'm fading with her. There'll be nothing left of us...nothing left of me...nothing left of the shards...*

No.

Wait.

His thoughts came slower and slower, as if every notion had to fight its way through thickening clouds and darkness, and would soon drown in the waters rising all around. The shards of Excalibur would not allow themselves to dissolve into nothingness. They had power, more than enough power to ensure they survived. Ariane had them with her, somewhere in this darkness, this howling storm. And Wally...Wally had his own connection to them. He could sense them, they influenced his emotions, sometimes he could even draw on their power, when he had to fight.

Could he draw on it now?

He had to focus. Had to concentrate. He fought through the thickening darkness and fog, searching, searching...

...and suddenly, there they were.

They shone in his mind, two bright stars, hard as diamond, impervious to the dissolution threatening to claim Ariane, threatening to claim Wally. He drew hungrily on their power, on their razor-edged reality, and felt himself coming back together, his mind sharpening, his senses strengthening. He could feel Ariane again, now, her "hand" slack in his, but still there. She hadn't dissolved completely, not yet, and he wasn't going to let that happen to her.

It. Would. Not. Happen. *Could* not, because Wally had another power to draw on, a power greater than the power of the shards, the same power Ariane had drawn on to race faster than she'd ever been able to before, had ever even thought possible before, across the breadth of North America to rescue her mother from Major's thugs. She'd told him how she'd found out that day that she could do more with the Lady's gift than she'd ever imagined, and that the power she'd drawn on had been...

Love. Ariane loved her mom, and love had given her wings.

And Wally...Wally loved Ariane.

He'd loved her before she'd realized – or admitted – she loved him. He loved her with all his heart and soul and being, and that love hadn't faded with his body, or hers. He could feel that love burning inside him, as though his heart had turned to flame, and he drew on it hungrily. With all the extra strength he could draw from the shards of the sword, he poured his love into the fading sense of

Ariane's presence, calling to her, begging her to come back to him, to come back to the light and warmth of his love, to leave the cool seductive world of mist and water...

...and she responded. She *brightened*. It was as though a light suddenly shone all around the two shards, lighting up the fog. He couldn't see her, he'd never been able to see her in this strange realm of the Lady's power, but her hand suddenly felt strong and solid in his once more, and then the shards blazed in his mind like twin suns as she suddenly reached out to them and drew power from them...

...and just like that, they were back in their bodies, bursting to the surface of dark water beneath a star-spangled sky. Wally gasped air, found mud beneath his feet on which to stand, and rose dripping to turn toward Ariane...

...only to see her fall backwards into the water with an enormous splash, unconscious.

Or dead.

CHAPTER SIX

HOME SWEET HOME

ARIANE CAME AWAKE bit by bit, as though the pieces of her consciousness were Lego blocks being locked together by a not-very-bright child. First, she realized she was lying on something far harder than her bed at Barringer Farm. Then she realized that she was cold. Then she realized that she was wet...and then she remembered that she was *never* wet anymore, unless she chose to be.

Then she realized that only part of her was cold, that in fact her back was warm, and *then* she realized that someone was lying curled up with her, arms around her chest, and *then* she realized who that had to be, and *then*, suddenly, she was fully awake.

She opened her eyes. Grey pre-dawn light filtered through a screen of branches. Beyond the foliage, grass sloped down to grey water, lapping at the shore. She looked farther out over the water, and saw an island, just visible in morning mist. There was something very familiar about it...

...and now she knew exactly where she was.

She was lying under the bushes on the shore of Wascana Lake in Regina, not a hundred metres from where the Lady of the Lake had first appeared to her and Wally, and Wally was lying with her, embracing her from behind.

But how had she...they...gotten there?

Her mind felt fuzzy and unfocussed, as if she'd been sick. She remembered Scotland. She and Wally had sneaked up to the castle...Wally had gone inside...

Flish. She'd grabbed Flish. But she hadn't been able to move her the way they'd intended, hadn't been able to spirit her away. And then Rex Major had shown up. He'd...shot her?

No...there'd been no gunshot...

But she remembered pain in her neck, whirling sickness, slipping down into darkness even as she dissolved into the magical watery realm through which they travelled, even as she pulled Wally with her...

He drugged me, she realized. *Merlin drugged me!*

The shards still pressed to her size blazed with the fury she felt. Wally stirred uneasily, and then suddenly his arms tightened. "Ariane?" he whispered. "Are you awake?"

She put one of her hands on his, and squeezed. "Yes," she whispered back. "We're in Regina."

"I know." His arms tightened even more, so tight she found it hard to breathe. "I thought...Ariane, I thought you were dead. Or dying. I didn't know what to do."

"Merlin shot me, didn't he?" she said. Her neck still hurt, a sharp, localized pain. She kept whispering, even though no one could possibly hear them. It was still very early in the morning. "Drugged me somehow?"

"Tranquilizer dart," Wally said. "Just as we were leaving. It was...Ariane, I thought you were going to fade away...disappear...and take me with you. I could feel you slipping into nothingness, I could feel myself dissolving. It was...terrifying. The most terrifying thing I've ever gone through."

Ariane felt sick. Every time she used the power, she felt

the seductive pull of the water, its constant urging to let herself go, to let herself become one with the rain and mist and streams and lakes, to abandon her individuality, her mind, her soul, her body. She'd learned to shut out that siren call, but it took a conscious effort every single time, and if she'd lost consciousness just as she dissolved...

She shuddered involuntarily, and Wally hugged her even tighter.

"Can't...breathe..." she gasped out.

"Sorry!" he said, and loosened his grip. But he didn't stop hugging her, and for that she was deeply grateful.

"How...how did we survive?" Ariane said. "I know it wasn't anything I did."

"I could feel the shards," Wally said. "Just like you've always said, they won't let themselves be destroyed that way. They gave me something to hang on to. And then I reached out for you."

"Reached out how?" Ariane said, but she suddenly realized she already knew, that she could feel the truth inside her, within the Lady's power – a link to Wally that hadn't been there before, a link like the one she shared with her mother. She could never again lose her mom, could always go to her in an instant, and now she had that same connection to Wally, and her throat constricted and her heart speeded even before she heard his answer.

"Love," Wally whispered. "I couldn't let you go. I couldn't let you vanish into nothingness. And so...I didn't."

Ariane squeezed his hand on her chest as tightly as he had hugged her a moment before.

"Ow," he said, but not as if he meant it.

It was several seconds before Ariane was able to speak around the lump in her throat. "But...how did we end up in Regina?" she finally managed. "I wasn't alert. I couldn't have brought us here consciously."

"You definitely didn't," Wally said. "You keeled over the moment you were solid again. You still had that damned dart in your neck. I pulled it out and threw it away and then I had to drag you out of the water. At first I thought..." His voice broke, just a little; he cleared his throat and tried again. "At first I thought you were dead. But you were breathing. I thought about trying to get an ambulance, but then I realized I couldn't, unless it was absolutely necessary. They'd identify you, and enter you into the computer, and in the hospital you'd be a sitting duck for Merlin. And after what he just did to you..." Ariane felt anger flowing from the shards, but not to her. "He tried to kill you."

"I doubt that," Ariane said. "He doesn't dare. He was probably just trying to knock me out. He tried once before, or his men did, in Gravenhurst, with chloroform, remember? He knows if I'm unconscious, I can't use my powers."

"Why are you defending him?" Wally said, almost angrily.

"I'm not!" Ariane said, and heard the snap in her own voice. *The shards*, she thought. "I'm not," she repeated, this time working hard to keep her voice soft. "I'm just trying to understand him. He wants the shards. If I had... vanished...he couldn't be sure he'd ever find them."

"Maybe," Wally said. "Or maybe he expects they'll just drop out of the sky and he can scoop them up at his leisure. With two shards in your possession and him out of the way, don't you figure *you* could find the rest pretty easily?"

Ariane hadn't thought of that – and she should have. The tranquilizer clearly wasn't entirely out of her system.

"I don't think I can take us anywhere," she said. "After what happened. I have to make sure this stuff has completely worn off. And I don't think it has."

"Can you at least get us dry?' Wally said. "My front is

warm enough, thanks to you, but my rear is freezing."

"Funny, I have the opposite problem," Ariane said. "I'll try."

She concentrated, and reached for the power...and the world whirled and spots danced in front of her eyes and she thought for a moment she was going to throw up. "Urgh," she said. "No. Not yet."

"Well, we can't lie here," Wally said. "Some fitness freak out for an early-morning jog is likely to find us and then our reputations will be shot."

Ariane laughed. "Somehow, I doubt our reputations matter anymore."

"All the same, can you walk?"

"I don't know," Ariane said. "Maybe. If you'll help me."

"Gee, I don't know..." Wally said, as though uncertain, then chuckled and gave her another quick squeeze. "Of course I'll help."

"But where will we go?"

"Home, sweet home," Wally said. "I still have a key. And it's only a few blocks away."

Wally's house was on Harrington Mews, a cul-de-sac just the other side of the Albert Street Bridge, only a bit over half a kilometre away. Wally climbed out from under the bush first, then held out his hand to Ariane. She sat up, and had to wait for the world to stop whirling; stood up, and promptly sagged against Wally. When they finally started walking, she had such a hard time moving in a straight line she knew anyone who saw them would be sure she was drunk. *There's another blow to my tottering reputation*, she thought, and snorted.

But no one saw them except a lone jogger – one of Wally's "fitness freaks" – and he paid no attention at all, lost in his own world of exercise and whatever tunes he was mainlining through his ear buds.

When they got to Harrington Mews, Wally led her around to the back fence of the house, right up against the dike bordering Wascana Creek, and through a gate, locked with a combination lock he made short work of. The back yard had been neatly cleaned of the usual winter detritus; though the Knights might not be using their family home, clearly they were still having someone look after it. Ariane wondered briefly if it might be Mrs. Carson, the housekeeper who had always favoured Flish over Wally, but she had a hard time picturing Mrs. Carson raking up decaying leaves.

"Hope they haven't changed the locks," Wally muttered as they made their way up onto the big deck. He looked around, confusion on his face. "Where are the deck furniture and the barbecue?"

"Probably moved into storage for the winter," Ariane said. "Can we get in, please? I'm c-cold." She didn't like not being able to wish herself dry, and even though it was spring, Regina mornings were chilly, and she didn't have Wally cuddled up close for warmth anymore.

"Sorry," Wally said, and unlocked the door.

He stepped inside...and stopped so suddenly Ariane ran into him.

"Oh, no," he whispered.

Ariane looked past him, and saw what he had seen... nothing.

The house was empty, not just of people, but of everything.

Wally Knight's family had moved out, and nobody had told Wally.

CHAPTER SEVEN

FAMILY HISTORY

FOR THE SECOND TIME in just a few hours, Wally's world dissolved into whirling chaos – but this chaos was in the physical world, not in the magical realm of the Lady of the Lake.

Ariane all but forgotten, he moved down the short hall. The house echoed weirdly. The kitchen was empty except for the appliances, the sugar and flour containers that had stood under the cabinet for his entire life gone, the dish rack gone, everything gone.

The living room was a sea of empty carpet, round depressions marking where furniture had rested for years, the walls bare except for a few discoloured patches and nail holes where pictures had hung.

He raced up the stairs, even though he knew what he would find.

The door to his room stood open.

There was nothing inside it.

His computer, his books, his clothes, his posters, his bed – everything had vanished as though it had never been.

Flish's room was just as empty, and his parents', and the bathroom. He trudged back down the stairs. Ariane sat on the third step from the bottom, there being nowhere else to sit. He felt guilty for having abandoned her.

But then, there was a lot of that going around. "It's all gone," he said. He knew she already knew it, but he still felt he had to say it out loud, as if saying it out loud would somehow help it seem more real. "All my stuff. All *our* stuff. It's not our house anymore."

He suddenly thought of something, and crossed the bare carpet to the living room window. He peered out through the blinds and saw what he would have seen right away if they'd come in the front – a *FOR SALE* sign, bearing the name and phone number of a prominent Regina realtor.

He let the blinds close again then walked back to Ariane, sitting down beside her on the steps. She put her hand on his knee. "Wally, I'm so sorry."

"I always thought that old joke was funny," Wally muttered.

Ariane gave him a bemused look. "What old joke?"

"About the parents writing the kid at university, telling him, 'You won't recognize the house when you come home – we've moved.' I guess I never really thought about it from the kid's perspective. It's not funny at all."

"You haven't been in touch with them," Ariane said softly. "You *couldn't* be in touch with them. They had no way to let you know. They didn't do it to hurt you."

"But they managed to all the same," Wally said glumly. "Well, at least it's warm and dry in here and nobody can see us. But there's another reason this is bad news."

Ariane's eyebrow lifted. "Worse than your family being scattered all over the world and the house you grew up in having been emptied and sold?"

Wally sighed. "Yeah. Grandma Knight's book is gone."

Ariane blinked. "I didn't know your grandmother was – is? – a writer."

"Was," Wally said. "She died five years ago. And she wasn't. A writer, I mean. Except for one book. She decided she wanted to collect all the family stories she could for her little boy – my dad."

"He was an only child?" Ariane asked. "Like me?" She sounded a little wistful, like she'd always wanted a sibling.

You want a sibling? Wally thought. *I'd gladly give you mine.* But out loud he said, "Yep. And her husband, my Grandpa Knight, was *also* an only child, whereas she had three brothers and a sister, so mostly the book was filled with stories from her side of the family, the Brays – tales of growing up on the prairies during the Depression."

Ariane laughed. "A very popular Saskatchewan-type book. I think one of my great aunts – one of my mom's aunts – wrote something like that."

"Fortunately, she also got a few stories from Grandpa Knight and his parents, my Great-Grandpa and Great-Grandma Knight. Apparently she got on really well with Great-Grandpa Knight; according to her, he doted on her because he'd always wanted a daughter as well as a son, and a daughter-in-law was almost as good."

"So did you read this book by your grandma?"

Wally nodded. "A long time ago. And only once. It was interesting, but not exactly *Harry Potter*. Grandma was a better cook than she was a writer." That was an understatement. Grandma's writing was so plodding a broken-down plough horse could have run circles around it.

"So why are you sorry it's not here now?" Ariane said. "Your parents won't have thrown it away. It will be in storage somewhere."

Wally shook his head. "It's worse than that. Finding it here was always a bit of a long shot, because I think there's a darn good chance Mom has it."

"In Scotland? Why?"

Wally hesitated. His hunch seemed far-fetched now – and

yet, what did they have to go on, except for far-fetched hunches? "Do you remember that night at Aunt Phyllis's, back when all this started, when I mentioned my great-grandfather Knight had been one of the infamous 'bachelors' at Cannington Manor?"

Ariane looked blank. "Um...no? And also...bachelors?"

"It was the night we saw the newspaper headline that made us realize Rex Major was going to Thunderhill Diamond Mine in the Northwest Territories."

Ariane laughed. "Well, I remember *that*, but not anything about your great-grandfather being a bachelor. Presumably he didn't stay one since he ended up being your great-grandfather."

"Great-grandfather Knight immigrated to Cannington Manor just before the turn of the century," Wally said. "A lot of the young single men who came to Cannington Manor were sent over from Britain because they didn't have any inheritance at home. The locals called them 'the bachelors.' Supposedly, they were there to learn to farm. Of course, being young and single and away from home, they weren't very interested in farming. They were mostly interested in partying."

Ariane sighed. "In other words, boys haven't changed in more than a century."

Wally laughed. "Grandma's book had a couple of stories Great-Grandpa Knight told her about the shenanigans the bachelors got up to, but I doubt he told her the half of it."

Ariane gave him a look. "Shenanigans?"

Wally laughed again. "Grandma's word, not mine. Anyway, never mind that. He also told her a very different kind of story. She asked him why he came to Canada, and he told her it wasn't for any of the usual reasons. He was very mysterious about it, but he claimed he had brought along some kind of family treasure he had to keep safe."

"Family treasure?" Ariane said dubiously. "What kind of treasure?"

"Great-Grandpa never told Grandma that. But Ariane, listen..." He told her what his mom had told him, in the Great Hall of Castle MacPhaiden, about how strange their family history was, with the Knights and MacPhaidens intermarrying over and over, down through the ages. "If Flish and I are heirs of Arthur – what if it comes from *both* sides of our family? What if the same magic that made sure you and I were in the same place at the same time when the Lady of the Lake popped up in Wascana Lake made sure those two families stayed tightly connected, century after century?" He leaned closer to her. "And what if they passed along something else – a treasure that had nothing to do with gold or silver, but a treasure given to them for safekeeping by a certain Lady of our acquaintance?"

Ariane's eyes widened. "You think this 'treasure' might be the hilt of Excalibur?"

"Yes," Wally said. "What else *could* it be? It certainly isn't the Holy Grail, which is what Mom's thinking. But she doesn't know anything about me and Flish being heirs of Arthur, or the Lady of the Lake or Merlin being going concerns in the twenty-first century."

Ariane's expression slipped back to skepticism. "I don't know, Wally. It seems like a long shot. The Lady said she scattered the shards all over the world. She didn't say anything about giving one piece of it to Arthur's heirs."

"So? Giving one of the shards to someone else to keep hidden down through the centuries still counts as 'scattering,' doesn't it? She had the whole sword in her hand after Arthur died. If the legends are true, it was hurled into a lake, and a hand came up, grabbed it, and drew it down into the water again. After that, she broke it apart. She took the four pieces of the blade to the hiding places we've already found – the Northwest Territories, southern

France, New Zealand, the Caribbean. But what better way to hide the fifth piece than to make sure it was always on the move, always being taken to *new* hiding places by the people entrusted with it?"

He'd been doubtful himself when the notion had first come to him, but the more he thought about it, the more it made sense.

As much sense as anything to do with this quest did, anyway.

As much sense as finding his house empty.

"Even if you're right – I'm not saying you are, but *if* you are – I'm not sure what good it does us," Ariane said. "Suppose your great-grandfather brought the hilt to Saskatchewan. Cannington Manor doesn't really exist anymore, does it? Nobody lives there."

"No," Wally said. "It's a provincial park. A heritage site. There's a church and a cemetery, a few old buildings, some museum-type stuff – old furniture, things like that – and a bunch of holes in the ground."

"You've been there?"

"Once, about four years ago. Great-Grandpa and Great-Grandma Knight are buried there."

"So how do we figure out where your great-grandfather hid whatever it is he hid?"

"That's why I want to look at Grandma's book," Wally said. "It might have something in it I've forgotten. But…" He spread his arms to indicate the empty house.

"If your mom has it, we could go back to Scotland and you could ask her if you could have a look," Ariane said, but she didn't sound very certain that was a good idea.

Wally, on the other hand, was very certain it *wasn't*. "No," he said firmly. "I changed the subject the minute she mentioned Great-Grandpa Knight because I didn't want Flish to think what I was thinking. If I ask Mom *anything* about it, it will be like sending up a flare to alert Rex

Major. Mom will tell him everything I say to her. She has to. She's under his Command. So is Dad." *Maybe I could get him to Command them to get back together*, he thought, and then wished he hadn't. He had a feeling that thinking he could use magic to force people to do whatever he wanted was a *very* bad habit to get into for someone who might very soon be wielding Excalibur.

"So we don't ask," Ariane said. "We sneak into her hotel room, like we did Major's in Yellowknife."

Wally thought about that, and felt himself grin. "I like the way you think," he said. "But we'll have to be very careful. If we find the book, we can't take it. That might alert Major to what we're searching for, too. We can only look at it. And we have to do it without Mom finding out for the same reason – she'll tell Merlin, and it won't be hard for him to put two and two together and figure out what interested us. And then…"

"Then we'd be in a race with him. Again." Ariane sighed. "I hope you're right about him not knowing anything about this already, Wally. Because if the race has already started, we're handicapped. I'm still in no shape to take us anywhere."

"I'd like to offer you a bed, or at least a couch, but…" Wally looked around the empty living room. "It looks smaller now than it used to," he murmured.

"Everything looks smaller when it's empty," Ariane said.

Wally blinked at her. "What?"

Ariane laughed. "It sounded good before I said it. Look, I can manage without sleep, but I can't manage without food. And caffeine seems like a really good idea, too. Caffeine and carbs. Let's go find a coffee shop."

"How about the Human Bean?" Wally said. "For old time's sake."

"The last time we went to the Human Bean, one of Major's henchmen jumped us," Ariane pointed out.

"Ancient history," Wally said. "That poor guy's still in jail for breaking into your bedroom. It'll be perfectly safe."

"Fine," Ariane said. "The Human Bean it is."

Wally stood up. "We'll go through the back yard again. Don't want anyone to see us coming out." He took another look around the empty house. Already it felt like someone else's, like an empty show home he'd wandered into.

But then, in some ways it hadn't really felt like home for a long time.

They went out the back door. "Hold up a sec," he told Ariane. He turned and closed the door, made sure it was locked, then leaned down and slid his key under it, giving it a good shove so it couldn't be seen.

"Are you sure about that?" Ariane said softly.

"Yeah," Wally said. "I'm sure. Come on." He turned his back on the house he'd grown up in, and walked away without looking back.

◄► ►►

The wet road to Inverness slipped by under the Jaguar's wheels. Merlin glanced at Felicia, who was staring out the passenger-side window, forehead against the glass, her breath rhythmically fogging it. *So it's moody teenager time again, apparently.* "Tell me exactly what you and Wally and your mother talked about," he said, as much to pass the time – it was a good hour's drive to the city – as because he thought he'd learn anything useful. He'd question Felicia's mother with the Voice of Command that evening anyway.

"It doesn't matter," Felicia said sullenly.

"Humour me," Major said, with just a flicker of anger, wishing for the umpteenth time he could Command the girl the way he could her parents; but then, if he'd been able to do that it would have meant she wasn't an heir of Arthur, she'd be no use to him at all, and they wouldn't be having this conversation.

If you could call it a conversation.

Felicia sighed so heavily the whole window fogged for a moment, but she didn't turn around. "Wally tried to convince me you're the devil and you're leading me to hell, Mom tried to convince both of us we should just kiss and make up and all go down to the village to get ice cream, and then for some reason Wally started bugging Mom about this stupid film project."

That caught Merlin's attention. "Bugging her how?"

"He just wanted to know about it. Mom went into this long explanation about how weird our family is, Knights and MacPhaidens marrying each other down through history, all that crap. God, I wish I'd been born into a normal family." Felicia traced an aimless pattern on the misted glass with her finger.

Merlin's eyes narrowed. If Wally was that interested, maybe his wild-goose chase wasn't so wild after all. He still hoped to find, when he got back to Toronto, that Ariane had conveniently dissolved into nothingness – and taken Wally with her – and he could take his time recovering her two shards from wherever they had fallen, then easily locate the hilt. But he knew from bitter experience how adept Ariane and Wally were at wriggling out from under his thumb just when he was about to squash them, and so it wouldn't hurt to continue to explore all other avenues to finding the hilt.

"What *exactly* did Wally show interest in?" he said. "Think hard, it's important."

Felicia shrugged. "Something about Great-Grandpa Knight."

"What about him?" Merlin said, trying very hard, and *almost* succeeding, not to let his impatience colour his voice.

Felicia sighed. "Great-Grandpa Knight was nutty as a fruitcake," she said. "Apparently he told Grandma that he'd had to leave Scotland to protect some sort of family secret, and that he'd brought a treasure with him. Mom's convinced he thought he had the Holy Grail."

"No," Merlin said absently, mind racing. "I know where the Grail is, and it's definitely not in Saskatchewan." He pulled out to pass a lorry. When he was back in his own lane, he said, "Change of plans. I'm going to fly to Toronto on my own. You're going to rejoin your mother."

Felicia jerked upright and her head snapped toward him, eyes blazing. "I am *not!*"

"Yes," Major said. "You are." He saw a turnoff for a village coming up; he slowed, turned into it and swung the Jaguar around, turning onto the road to head back the way they'd come just as the lorry he'd passed minutes before roared by, the driver giving him an unfriendly look. He accelerated back toward Castle MacPhaiden.

"I told Mom I was leaving!" Felicia shouted. "I stormed off. I can't go back!"

"You'll do as I tell you!" Major snapped, patience worn thin at last. He glanced at the girl, her hair still hanging wet and lank around her shoulders, that ridiculous black dress clinging damply. "I've given you everything you've wanted, these past few months. That necklace, that dress, those shoes, and dozens more of each. As much spending money as you want. Parties. Rich boys to flirt with."

He let his voice sharpen, like a swordsman revealing just an inch or two of steel to emphasize he was armed and dangerous. "But remember this, Felicia Knight – *I can take it all away.* I can make you a virtual prisoner in my condo if I choose. Anyone you might think to complain to, I can buy off or simply Command to ignore you. You will do as I tell you, or your little I'm-a-celebrity fantasy will come to a very abrupt end."

Felicia's nostrils flared. "You wouldn't dare," she snarled. "You *need* me. I'm an heir to Arthur. You can't use your precious shards without my help."

"*Need* you?" Merlin drew his verbal sword a little more. "Don't give yourself airs, little girl. Your help is desirable, yes – but never, *ever* think you're invaluable. I did not even know heirs to Arthur still existed when I began this. Yes, having you at my side will make my conquest of Earth and Faerie easier, but make no mistake – once I have the complete sword I will have power enough to open the door into Faerie and carry out my plans for its liberation with or without you. Annoy me enough now, or keep crossing me, and 'without you' will come to seem a very attractive option. *Do you understand me?*"

Felicia's lips pressed together so tightly they turned white. She nodded, once.

"Good." Major sheathed his metaphorical blade and instead let a smile flicker across his face "Good. So. To reiterate. You will return to your mother. You will find out everything you can about your great-grandfather Knight and his treasure. Especially, you will try to find out where he hid it. The moment you know that, you will phone me. And if I am satisfied with what you tell me in that phone call, *then* I will send for you and you may return to Toronto. Clear?"

Felicia nodded, once. Then she turned her back on him, folded her arms across her chest, and stared out into the rain-swept Scottish countryside again.

"Sulk all you want, child," Merlin said to her back. "Just do what I tell you."

A sign flashed by. Twenty kilometres back to Castle MacPhaiden.

They drove the rest of the way in silence broken only by the rhythmic thumping of the windshield wipers.

CHAPTER EIGHT

THE LAIRD OF CASTLE MacPHAIDEN

AFTER A BREAKFAST SANDWICH of egg and ham and cheese on an English muffin, plus a very large coffee and a cinnamon bun, Ariane felt, if not exactly on top of the world, at least able to once more magically transport people around it.

The tranquilizer Rex Major had shot her with had to have been powerful stuff to have knocked her out almost instantly. She wondered exactly how that worked, when she'd immediately dematerialized into the clouds. It couldn't have circulated through her bloodstream when she didn't have a body. Or could it?

Maybe it just started to take effect as I dematerialized, then asserted itself again the minute we rematerialized, she thought. *That would explain why I passed out the second we hit Wascana Lake, and why it's taking so long for it to wear off completely.*

She supposed that made sense. Their clothes dematerialized and rematerialized with them, after all, as did backpacks and the shards themselves, so presumably anything in her bloodstream would do the same.

She shuddered. If not for the fact that killing her directly would apparently somehow destroy Excalibur forever, she was certain the tranquilizer pistol would have been a real gun.

She wondered what Rex Major thought had happened to them after they dematerialized. Did he think they'd simply vanished into the fog, the shards dropping out of the clouds to land wherever they happened to be when they disappeared forever? Did he believe Ariane and Wally were dead, and all his troubles were over?

Possibly, but they couldn't count on it.

They had no clue where Major was now, or Felicia. From Wally's description of his conversation with his sister, as he ate a white-chocolate-and-saskatoon-berry scone and downed a giant mocha latte, it seemed unlikely Felicia had stayed with their mother. Which might at least make it a little less likely that she or Major would twig to what Ariane and Wally were up to, if they carried out their plan to break into Jessica Knight's hotel room.

The trouble was, of course, they had no idea where that hotel room might be, other than "somewhere in Scotland," which wasn't much help. It was presumably not too far from Castle MacPhaiden, but there hadn't been any place to stay in the nearest village, unless you counted the rooms over the pub, and neither Ariane nor Wally thought it likely Jessica Knight and her crew would settle for those.

"We don't dare call her," she pointed out to Wally as she came back to their table by the window with her refilled coffee cup. The more caffeine the better, this morning.

They had the Human Bean almost to themselves. It was still pretty early and the grabbing-coffee-on-the-way-to-work-or-school crowd hadn't arrived yet. An elderly man sat at a corner table reading a book, and the two baristas had vanished into the back room. The Eagles' *Hotel California* played in the background.

"I agree," Wally said. "But it's still only early afternoon

in Scotland. She'll still be at the castle. If we go back there, I can see her again. But this time, Flish won't be around."

"Are you sure about that?"

"The way she stormed off? I'm sure," Wally said confidently. "I won't ask Mom anything about family history, so she won't tell Major what I'm interested in. But at least I should be able to find out where she's staying. Then tonight…"

"Not the most solid of plans," Ariane said doubtfully. "You don't even know if she has your grandmother's book with her."

"I know it's a long shot, Ariane," Wally said, "but it's the only shot we have at the moment. Unless the shards are telling you anything about the hilt's location?"

Ariane sighed. They weren't, of course. No more than they had for months. Wherever the hilt of Excalibur was, it was beyond the reach of the Lady's magic. Perhaps hidden in salt water, as it had been on Cacibajagua Island, or somewhere with no water at all. The desert, maybe? "No," she said.

"Well, then," Wally said. He finished off his scone and wiped his fingers on a napkin, then wiped his mouth. He put the napkin down on the table. "Do we stop in at Barringer Farm before we go?"

Ariane wanted to say yes – wanted to talk to Mom and Aunt Phyllis and Emma – but what good would it do? They'd just worry, and every time they were in contact with the three women, they put them in more danger. If Major ever figured out where they'd been hiding all these months…

So instead she shook her head. "No," she said. "Let's just go. If this really does pan out, maybe we'll have the hilt by evening and this will all be over."

"Right," Wally said. "Could happen." But he didn't really sound as if he believed it. He looked around, taking in the mostly empty coffee shop. "I think we can risk going into the bathroom together."

Ariane nodded. They got up from the table and walked to the hallway at the back of the brightly painted shop. The coast was clear as they opened the door, but just as they stepped inside the old man who had been reading in the corner appeared at the end of the hall. It was too late to hide. Ariane gave him a bright smile and then followed Wally into the bathroom.

Well, she thought, *I didn't recognize him. He* probably *doesn't know who either of us are...*

Wally started the water running, then held out his hand to her. She took it, put her other hand into the stream, and took them both down the drain.

She knew at once she was in trouble.

The "caffeine and carbs" might have masked the effects of the tranquilizer, but the drug still clearly lingered in her system. She felt as if she were pushing her way through molasses, with Wally, a dead weight, slowing her even more. She never felt in danger of losing herself, not with Wally holding tight to her with his somehow both very real and yet immaterial hand, not with the new glimmering link, forged from love, tying her to him, and not with the two shards in her possession shining hard and bright in her senses. But she could tell *this* journey was not going to take mere minutes as the last trip to Scotland had. This one was going to take as long as – or longer than – their journeys before Cacibajagua Island, before she had realized how many of the limitations on her power were self-imposed.

Yet she had no choice but to struggle gamely onward, through lake and river and cloud. At least, with two shards and Wally to help her draw on them, she was never in danger of running out of power. But all the same, when at long, long last they rematerialized in the same small loch they had appeared in before, she almost passed out again as she had when they'd materialized in Wascana Lake, this time from sheer exhaustion.

Together they staggered out of the loch. The earlier rain had subsided to a fine drizzle, but she was in no shape to do anything about it, because she was too busy leaning over and throwing up the remains of her breakfast and coffee, which had dematerialized and rematerialized along with her body, only to end up in an ignominious jumble in the Scottish mud.

Wally lay flat on his back in the grass, panting. "I thought we'd never get here," he panted. "That was almost worse than last time."

"Tranquilizer...hadn't worn off completely after all," Ariane gasped out. She spat, then gathered up a handful of the loch water, managed to find just enough magic left in her to purify it, rinsed out her mouth, and spat again. It took about three rinses to get rid of the awful taste.

"How long did that take?" Wally said.

"It took hours," Ariane said. "Hours." She squinted up at the sky. "Long enough that I think it's getting dark."

"Getting dark?" Wally cried. He scrambled up. "That means it's late evening! Mom may have left the castle! Come on!"

Ariane followed him through the heather to the road leading to Castle MacPhaiden. Up there, atop the hill they'd already climbed once that day, lights had just begun to glow through the tall, narrow windows. She trudged through the mist, hoping desperately that whatever awaited them, it wouldn't require her to call on her magic.

At the moment, she felt about as magical as a haggis.

◄◄ ►►

As they laboured up the hill, Wally thought the best thing about finally completing – or even failing to complete – the quest for the shards of Excalibur would be never again having to be dissolved into water and reassembled somewhere else. The last two trips had stripped away any remaining wonder at the magic of it. And he hadn't been joking about the last one being almost worse than the one during which they'd both almost dissolved into nothingness. That time, he'd been desperately trying to save them both, so at least he'd been doing something. This time, he felt as though he had been dragged to Scotland behind a horse, and it had gone on...and on...and *on*. He ached all over, and he had the strangest feeling he was missing a few pieces. *How unusual, Mr. Knight*, he could just hear some future doctor telling him, *Someone seems to have stolen one of your kidneys.*

Which was why what had started out as a run up the hill to the castle had turned very quickly into dogged, tight-lipped plodding.

Ariane was clearly in no better shape. She might not have passed out on arrival this time, but she had very thoroughly and noisily puked up her breakfast, which had been almost enough to make him do the same.

He gulped. Better not to think about it.

Whatever we do, he thought, *we have to stop Rex Major from tranquilizing Ariane ever again.*

As if they'd have much say in the matter.

They finally reached the castle courtyard, only to find Wally's worst fears realized. The equipment van and his mother's rented car were gone, although at least Rex Major's black Jag wasn't there, either. The only vehicle was one he hadn't seen before, a rather spiffy silver-grey Sean-Connery-era-James-Bond Aston Martin, which made him think he was probably on the right track with his earlier thought that the owner of the castle might collect cars.

It was starting to get seriously dark now, and this far north, this time of the year, that meant it was late indeed.

But the fact there were lights in the castle, and a new car outside, must mean someone was home.

"What...what do we do?" Ariane panted, catching up to him. "There's no one here."

"Yes, there is," Wally said, pointing to the Aston Martin. Then he turned toward the castle. "I think the owners are back. Someone actually lives in this castle, remember. If what Mom said was true, probably even distant relations. Maybe they'll know where Mom is staying."

He took a step forward. Ariane grabbed his arm. "You can't just walk up to the door and knock!"

"Why not?" Wally said. "They're relatives – well, maybe. Anyway, have you got a better idea?"

Clearly she didn't; she sighed and let go of his arm.

He strode resolutely across the wet cobblestones to the stairs from which they had so nearly disastrously fled just a few hours earlier. Castle MacPhaiden, Wally had noted earlier, boasted a doorbell – certainly not part of the original equipment. He pushed it, and waited.

The walls were far too thick for him to hear whatever sound the bell made inside. For a moment nothing happened, and he wondered if he was wrong about someone being home. Then, suddenly, a lot of lights came on – not just on the porch, but all around the courtyard, which suddenly blazed as bright as day – brighter, in fact, than this grey day had been.

"Ow," Ariane said, throwing up her hand to shade her eyes.

"Security," Wally said. He grinned. "We should count ourselves lucky – in the old days castle security would have meant pouring boiling oil down on our heads."

Ariane gave him a look he'd become very familiar with over the past few months – he thought of it as the "stop being so Wallyish" look.

But he couldn't help being Wallyish if he tried, so he

just grinned even wider and turned back to face the door. He grinned at it, too, on the theory that anyone with that many lights outside the building was bound to also have security cameras, one of which must be trained on them right now. He glanced back at Ariane. She hadn't been expending any energy trying to keep them dry on the long walk up the hill, and as a result, she looked, quite adorably, like a half-drowned kitten. He doubted he looked anything like that cute, but he hoped he at least appeared harmless.

Apparently he did, because he heard the sound of the door being unbolted, and then it creaked open, revealing…

Wally had to work very hard not to let his grin turn into a laugh, because the man the opened door revealed looked like every Canadian's stereotypical image of a Scotsman – broad-shouldered, barrel-chested, red-haired and red-bearded. If only he'd been wearing a kilt he would have been perfect, but instead he wore khaki pants and a green pullover cardigan. Leather slippers encased his feet.

"Aye?" he growled at Wally. "What're you doing, troubling me this time of night? This castle is not open to the public even during the day." He had a thick Scots accent, though not as impenetrable as some Wally had heard, sometimes from people who had lived in Saskatchewan for decades.

"I'm Wally Knight, and this is Ariane Forsythe?" Wally said. "My mom is Jessica Knight, of Knight Errant Pictures? She was here shooting earlier today?" His voice had deepened alarmingly in recent months, but he did his best to sound as young as possible, and even though he detested up-talking, he swallowed his pride and tried to make everything sound like a question anyway.

The bearded man's face and voice softened perceptibly. "She's been gone these four hours, lad," he said. "Where have you been that you did not know that?"

"We…" Wally looked at Ariane. "We…went down to…" He couldn't remember the name of the village. In fact, he didn't think he'd ever known it. "…um, to the village." He dropped the up-talking; he couldn't keep it up and live with himself. "We thought she was going to pick us up there but she never showed up and we don't have cell phones and we thought maybe we'd misunderstood and we were supposed to go with Rex Major instead but he didn't show up either and then it got late and so we did the only thing we could think of and we walked all the way back up here. Through the rain." He tried to put just the tiniest of quivers in his voice, as if he might be about to cry but was too manly to show it. "Do…do you know where she went? We don't even know what hotel she's staying at!"

The man looked from Wally to Ariane and back again, and then sighed. "You'd best come in," he said. "I have your mother's contact information. We can call her and figure out what's to be done." He stepped to one side to let them pass. "My name is Alexander MacPhaiden," he added. "Call me Alex. If your mother is Jessica Knight, née MacPhaiden, than I expect we're distantly related."

He led them down the hallway Wally remembered from earlier that day, but opened the first of the closed doors Wally had passed to reveal a staircase leading up. At the top was another door, behind which lay the last thing Wally expected – a thoroughly modern apartment that could have been anywhere. The only things betraying the fact it was actually in a centuries-old castle were the narrow windows cut through the thick stone walls, showing only darkness beyond. Everywhere else, the stone walls were hidden behind regular drywall painted pale green.

Alex laughed at Wally's expression. "Expecting something a bit more medieval, lad?"

"I guess I was," Wally admitted.

Alex grinned. "Believe me, if the old lairds of the castle had had central heating and insulation, they would have installed them, too. Today was a rather fine day by local standards. And the winters…brrr."

I'm from Saskatchewan, Wally thought about pointing out, but stayed quiet instead – *a first time for everything!* – and just kept looking around.

On closer inspection, he spotted a *few* other hints that this modern apartment was really on the top floor of a centuries-old castle. A suit of armour stood in one corner, right next to the big-screen TV. Crossed swords and a shield hung over the low, sleek chrome-and-black leather couch. The huge fireplace was lined with massive stones, blackened over centuries. And above it hung a very old painting, showing…

Whoa!

Alex was saying something to Ariane, but Wally wasn't listening, all his attention suddenly focussed on the old work of art. He walked over to the fireplace and stared up at the painting. It wasn't very big, maybe sixty-by-sixty centimetres, and the varnish had darkened to the point the original colours could barely be guessed at, but what it showed…

…what it showed was a woman dressed in white, standing half-submerged in the waters of a lake, holding out the hilt of a broken sword to a man in armour, kneeling on the shore.

"What is this?" Wally asked, interrupting whatever Alex had been saying to Ariane – something about making tea.

Alex came over to the hearth. "It's an old family legend, that is. The painting dates from the early 1800s, but that's just some artist's interpretation. The legend is much, much older."

"What's the legend?" Wally barely breathed.

Alex gave him a curious look. "Well, the story goes that

the MacPhaidens were entrusted with a great treasure by none other than the Lady of the Lake – of the King Arthur legend, you know – herself." Alex laughed. "All nonsense, of course. I think every Scottish family has some old legend attached to it, and half of them have to do with King Arthur. Strangely enough, since if he was real he most likely operated more in Wales and Cornwall."

"What treasure?" Wally said, trying to keep his voice casual but not really succeeding too well. "It looks like the hilt of a sword."

"Aye, lad, that it is," Alex said. He deepened his voice so it boomed like a movie-trailer voice-over. "The MacPhaidens were given the timeless task of protecting the hilt of the great sword of King Arthur himself – Excalibur...bur...bur..." He let his voice echo away into portentous silence, then laughed. "Nonsense, as I said. How exactly we could have been entrusted with the hilt of an entirely fictional sword, I'm not quite sure."

"Where...where's the hilt supposed to be now?"

Alex laughed again. "That's the fun part, lad. It's supposed to be in Canada."

Wally's eyes slid past Alex to Ariane, who was following the conversation wide-eyed. "Has my mother seen this painting?"

Alex shook his head. "No, lad. I'll be showing it to her tomorrow during the interview."

"Interview?"

"Aye. I had to go to Inverness today, so we couldna do it this afternoon, but she said that was fine, she wanted to use the Great Hall to shoot her introductory narration. Tomorrow I'm to tell her all about the great Red Wedding, when our unsavoury ancestors seized control of this castle by killing the previous owners at a feast. Of course, most castles changed hands via bloodshed and treachery in those days, so I dinna think you can blame the

MacPhaidens overmuch."

Wally hesitated. He really wanted to ask Alex not to tell his mom about the painting, not to share with her the details of the legend that up until now she'd only heard hints of – but he couldn't think of any way to justify it. Which meant that tomorrow his mom would hear that the mysterious MacPhaiden artifact wasn't the Holy Grail at all, but the hilt of Excalibur, and while *she* wouldn't make much of that, Rex Major certainly would when next he questioned her using the Voice of Command.

More than ever, they needed to see Grandma Knight's book, and hope it gave some clue as to where the hilt had been hidden by her father-in-law.

"We'd better call Mom now," Wally said. "She'll...be worried."

"Aye, lad. As I said, I have her contact information here somewhere." He went to a sleek glass-topped computer desk with a brand-new Mac on it, and rummaged through a pile of papers.

Wally glanced at Ariane, who looked astonished that there actually seemed to be something to Wally's wild hunch. He allowed himself to feel a little smug.

"Here we are," Alex said, turning around with a sticky note in his hand. "She's at the Claymore Arms – that's a hotel in Clachgorm, two villages down the valley. I can run you over there if you like after you've talked to her."

"Clachgorm? Two villages down?" Wally said. "Could you...show us on a map?"

Alex blinked. "Sure lad, but why? I willna make you walk."

"I'd just like to...understand the geography better."

Alex shrugged. "Well, let's see..." He turned back to the desk, which held a shelf of books above the monitor. He ran his finger over the spines, found what he wanted, pulled down what appeared to be a local guidebook, flipped through it until he found a map, and then held it out open to Wally and Ariane. "We're here," he said, pointing out CASTLE MACPHAIDEN, "and south down the valley... here. The Claymore Arms in Clachgorm. Gets a special mention, even. Supposed to be haunted, you know."

"So's your castle," Wally pointed out.

Alex grinned. "Lots of strange noises here at night, sure enough," he said. "but considering the state of this pile's plumbing, I'm not surprised. I've never seen a ghost, unless you count the really pale grooms who show up for weddings after their stag nights, looking as though they'd very much prefer to be still in bed. Very popular place for weddings, is my Great Hall, though you wouldna think it would be, given its history." He closed the book and put it back on the shelf above the computer. "So, then, I'll give your mum a call to let her know you're all right, and drive you over there."

"No need," Wally said without thinking.

Alex frowned. "What?"

"I mean, no hurry," Wally said hastily, but that didn't sound right either, considering the story they'd come up with, so he rushed on to add, "what I mean is, could we... um, could I...have...get...a drink of water before we go?"

"Me, too," Ariane chimed in.

Alex blinked. "Aye, certainly. " He turned toward the kitchen. "I'll –"

"We can get it ourselves," Wally said quickly to forestall him. "While you call Mom."

Alex raised a bushy red eyebrow. "Well...all right. Tumblers in the cupboard above the sink." He turned to the phone, and Wally followed Ariane into the kitchen.

"You saw the map? You can get us there?" Wally whispered. Then he thought of something else. "Do you have enough strength?"

"'Aye,' to all three questions," Ariane said, and grinned

when he raised an eyebrow. "If there's water nearby, of course."

"This is Scotland, and it was raining all day," Wally said. "I don't think finding water will be a problem."

He reached out and turned on the tap. He glanced back into the living room. Alex had his back to them. "Not getting an answer," he called, and started to turn around.

But by the time he completed his turn, they were no longer there.

CHAPTER NINE

THE CLAYMORE ARMS

CLACHGORM, THE VILLAGE in which the Claymore Arms was situated, was only small, rather than miniscule like the one nearest Castle MacPhaiden. It boasted an ornamental fountain in the town square, the surrounding pool of which had just enough water in it for Ariane to materialize them.

Despite her assurances to Wally that she had strength enough for the short jaunt, she felt, as they climbed out of the pool into the fortuitously empty square, that she'd had just *barely* enough. Now she really did need sleep. And food.

Especially food.

The Claymore Arms wasn't hard to find – not only was it just a couple of blocks from the town square, it was the largest building in Clachgorm. While the bottom floor looked as old as everything else in the town, the upper two storeys looked as if they'd been bought at a no-name department store and assembled from a big yellow box simply labelled *HOTEL*.

Ariane and Wally stood in a dark alley across from the hotel's main entrance, a wooden door on a stone porch in the old part of the structure, fractured light shining through the tiny diamond panes of the large windows to either side. The faint sound of laughter and glasses and clinking cutlery carried across the street through the cool night air.

Someone's having food, Ariane thought. *No fair!* Her stomach growled.

Wally glanced at her, and she realized to her embarrassment he'd heard it. "You must be hungry," he said. "*I'm* hungry, and I didn't throw up my breakfast on arrival."

Ariane grimaced. "Don't remind me." She tried to ignore the siren sounds of dining and focus instead on the task at hand. "What's the plan? It's late. Your mom's probably in her room."

"So we need to get her out of it." He frowned. "You know, it doesn't matter if she knows I'm here. I can go to her room, tell her I'm starving, have her take me down to the dining room – and make sure the door doesn't lock behind us, so you can get in. You can look for the book. It will be in her briefcase, most likely, or even out on the desk with her computer."

"What if I can't find it?"

"Then we'll come up with another plan," Wally said. "As a last resort I'll ask her about it, but that'll send up a red flag for Rex Major and I'm really *really* hoping he hasn't made the connection between the hilt and the MacPhaiden family yet."

Ariane chewed her lip. "All right," she said. "But just one thing."

"What?"

"If she takes you to the dining room, get me a doggy bag."

Wally laughed. "Promise." He took another look at the hotel. "I'll go in first. They probably won't tell me what room's she's in; I'll have to call her from the lobby. Come in right after me but don't stand too close; stand by the stairs – or the elevator if there is one – and as I pass you I'll let you know what room she's in. You can wait until you see us coming down to the dining room, then go up. There won't be any rush if we're eating."

"Okay. Um…why does it matter if anyone sees us come in together? Nobody knows who we are."

Wally grinned. "It probably doesn't. But we're in Scotland. James Bond was born here. And we *are* facing a supervillain bent on taking over the world, so…why not a little Bondian intrigue just to keep things interesting?"

Ariane sighed. *Boys!* No, that wasn't fair. *Wally!* "All right."

"Right, then. Here goes." Wally looked both ways along the street, although there hadn't been a car in all the time they'd stood there, then crossed the cobblestones, still shining wet from the day's rain. He disappeared through the big wooden door.

Ariane waited a few minutes, and then followed him.

The lobby of the hotel looked about as she'd expected – lots of dark wood, heavy beams in the low ceiling, big leather chairs, crossed swords above the enormous fireplace. A smell of roasting meat that made Ariane's mouth water came from the left, through a heavy-timbered arch, while from the other direction came much coarser talking and laughter; presumably, the pub.

Wally stood at the desk, talking on a white courtesy phone. He put it down, and walked toward the stairs. "306," he said as he passed her.

Well, that's easy to remember, Ariane thought. It was the main Saskatchewan telephone area code.

Wally disappeared up the red-carpeted stairs. Ariane sat down in one of the big leather chairs by the fireplace and pretended to read an old copy of *The Scots Magazine*, which, she saw with some amazement, had first been published in 1739. The issue, from February, focussed mostly on Robbie Burns; other articles included an interview with Billy Connolly and something entitled "Ten things you cannae miss."

It was, she thought, the most Scottish thing she had ever seen.

She got so interested in the Billy Connolly interview that she almost missed the one thing she really didn't want to miss, which was Wally and his mom coming into the lobby. She watched them go into the dining room, and sighed, wishing she could follow them into that meat-scented heaven. But her task lay elsewhere.

Wally having placed the idea in her head, the James Bond movie theme played in the back of her mind as she trudged up the stairs to the third floor. She found Room 306 at the very end of the hall, which, like the outside of the upper two storeys, could have been in a Travelodge in Moose Jaw for all the Scottish character it displayed.

She wondered how Wally had managed to ensure the door wouldn't be locked. It certainly *looked* properly closed; but when she pushed, it swung inward without resistance and she saw a plastic bandage preventing it from latching shut.

Good thinking, Wally, she thought, impressed. Not that Wally Knight's resourcefulness should come as much of a surprise after everything they'd been through. How many times had he saved her or the quest by now? She'd lost count.

The room was surprisingly large, probably due to its being at the end of the hall. It had only one large bed, plus a couch, a couple of chairs, a coffee table, and, of course, a desk.

A stack of books and papers teetered on the coffee table. Ariane crossed to it, wishing she'd thought to ask exactly what "Grandma's book" looked like. But she supposed it wouldn't be too hard to recognize.

It certainly wasn't – it was right on top. *Family Stories of the Brays and the Knights*, read a label pasted on the outside of a black loose-leaf notebook.

Ariane picked up the notebook and started leafing through it. It consisted of typewritten pages, with a few yellowing photos hand-pasted here and there. Even though she had probably an hour before Wally and his mom came back from the dining room, she worried how hard it would be to find the story of Great-Grandpa Knight – but in fact it was in the very first chapter.

My husband's father, Ebenezer Alastair Knight... she read, and had to stop for a second right there. *Ebenezer? Really?* She shook her head and carried on. *...was from Scotland and came in 1892 to Cannington Manor where there was an attempt to make a proper British village, which didn't work so well on the Canadian prairie as you can imagine! He was one of what they called the bachelors because they were young unmarried men which mostly accounts for why they did more carousing and drinking than they ever did learning to farm like they were supposed to but fortunately for my husband and eventually me he didn't stay a bachelor he met my husband's mother a nice German girl Laura Umstattd in Carlyle one day in 1901 and they got married within six months they hit it off so fast.*

Ebenezer told a lot of stories about the days in Cannington Manor like the time he and Peter Prescott went out to the Beckton Brothers' big house called Didsbury in a wagon to go fishing and had a little too much to drink on the way and got stuck in the mud and had to... Ariane skimmed over that one, and a couple of other stories of what had passed for outlandish "shenanigans" – sure enough, Grandma had called them that – more than a hundred years ago. Then her eye was caught by the word "treasure," and she paid closer attention again.

Ebenezer told me he hadn't really come to Saskatchewan to learn to farm he had come because he had a secret treasure he had to keep hidden away though he never told me from whom.

Funny Grandma Knight knew when to use "whom" but couldn't punctuate, Ariane thought, then felt a little guilty; Grandma Knight had probably had no more than an eighth-grade education in a one-room school. She kept reading.

He never would say what the treasure was just said it was something that had belonged to his Mama whose maiden name was Eleanor MacPhaiden and rightly a MacPhaiden should have it but it had come to him. Then he said he'd already hidden the treasure away where no one would find it but someday he'd be with it again. I asked him many times what it was but he never did say right up until his dying day which came in 1946 and although he lived in Weyburn by then he was buried back in Cannington Manor in the cemetery of All Saints Anglican Church where he used to attend and about the only thing left of the old town to this day and when my mother-in-law Laura died six years later she was buried there too.

But I'm getting ahead of myself because here I am talking about Ebenezer's funeral and I haven't even told you about when I met him when James took me to his folks to meet them. That was in...

Ariane closed the book, heart pounding. A MacPhaiden family treasure. Wally was right – it *had* to be the hilt of Excalibur!

She carefully put the book down on the coffee table again, trying to make it look exactly as it had before. She'd go down to the dining room, catch Wally's eye, give him a sign, they could talk again, figure out their next move...

"Hello, bitch," came an all-too-familiar voice from behind her. Ariane's heart skipped a beat, then she turned to face the new arrival standing in the just-opened door.

Flish!

◄◄ ►►

Wally had been terrified the last time he'd spoken to his mom. He discovered as he climbed the stairs of the Claymore Arms that nothing had changed. If anything, it was worse this time. From her point of view, he'd run out of the Great Hall to retrieve Flish and simply never come back. She must have been frantically worried about him ever since. How could he explain where he'd been for the past few hours?

She didn't answer the phone when Alex called, he reminded himself as he paused at the top of the stairs to take a plastic bandage out of the first-aid kit in his backpack, tucking it into his pocket so it would be handy. *She might not even be in there. In which case we can just figure out a way to break in, and...*

But when he knocked on the door of Room 306, he heard her call, "Who is it?"

He cleared his throat. "It's Wally, Mom."

Dead silence for an instance. Then he heard a rustle on the other side of the door – probably Mom peeking through the peephole. That was followed by an audible gasp, almost a shriek, and then the door was flung open.

"Wally!" Mom grabbed him and hugged him. "It is you! Oh, God, Wally, I thought you were dead, I haven't heard anything since you called your father that one time, and that was months ago!"

Wait, what? "But, Mom," Wally said cautiously, "you saw me at the castle."

"Castle?" she said, her voice muffled. She straightened. "No, I didn't...do you mean you saw me at Castle MacPhaiden? You were *there?*"

Wally's mind raced. "Have you talked to Rex Major recently?"

Mom straightened, wiping her eyes. "Why, yes, he called me a little while ago – he's flying back to Toronto and wanted to make sure I have everything I need for this project of mine he's funding. Why?"

"I...saw him at the castle," Wally said. "That's why I didn't come to you there. I didn't want him to see me."

Half of that was true, at least.

Mom clearly had no memory of their earlier meeting, of the argument with Flish, of him running out after her into the rain, and therefore of him not coming back. That could only mean one thing:

Rex Major had heard her account of it, and then Commanded her to forget.

Anger roared up inside him, and most of it was his, even though the shards were close enough, downstairs with Ariane, that he knew they were feeding it, too. But for once he welcomed the sword's bloodthirsty single-mindedness. *Kill your enemies*, that was Excalibur's solution to everything, and the thought of Rex Major forcing his mother to forget she'd already been reunited with her son made that solution seem like a pretty good one. *First head I lop off with Excalibur will be yours, Merlin,* Wally snarled silently. A part of him recoiled from that, but it was a much smaller part than it used to be.

The phone rang. Mom ignored it.

"Aren't you going to answer that?" Wally said. He was pretty sure he knew who it had to be – Alex MacPhaiden, worrying how he was going to explain to Wally's mom how her son had shown up on his doorstep with a girl and then vanished into thin air from his kitchen. Wally had been trying to come up with a lie to cover that, not surprisingly without much success. "We slipped out a secret passage you never even knew was there and managed to catch a ride with a guy who drove two hundred kilometres an hour," was the best he'd come up with.

Fortunately, he didn't have to put it to the test. Mom said, "Let it ring. You're more important. Where have you been? What's been happening to you?"

Wally sighed. They'd already had this conversation once, back in the castle, and he remembered it, even if his mom didn't. *Well, at last I'll be working from a script,* he thought. "I've got so much to tell you, Mom, but…can we go get something to eat? I'm starving. I've been…hitch-hiking, and I haven't had much money, and…"

"Oh, of course, Wally." Mom looked stricken. "I'll just grab my purse."

She turned back into the room, and Wally quickly went to the door. He pulled the plastic bandage from his pocket, pulled off the tabs, and slapped it over the door latch, and then held the door for his mom as she came back toward the hall, standing so she couldn't see what he'd done.

"Make sure the door closes, Wally," she said.

"I will." And, of course, it closed just fine…

…it just didn't latch.

They headed down the stairs. Ariane sat by the fire-place, apparently reading a magazine – okay, *really* reading a magazine; for a minute he thought he'd have to go over and tap her on the shoulder to get her attention –"Excuse me, miss, do you have a Scotch mint?" he'd say – but she looked up just in time. He let his gaze slide over her, and then followed his mother into the dining room, to once again carefully *not* explain exactly how and why he'd dis-appeared, and no doubt to once more hear how she blamed herself and how hard everything had been for everyone, and probably to tell him once again how won-derful Rex Major was being to Flish and what a great friend of the family he was, and he just hoped that at that point he didn't throw up, because he really was starving, and it would be an awful waste.

Thinking of starving – and also, unfortunately, of throwing up – made him think of Ariane. He wasn't sure exactly how he would justify to his mother asking for a doggie bag – was that what they called them here? – but he had to get food to Ariane somehow.

He wondered where Flish was. He'd been afraid he'd see her again, but if his mom wasn't mentioning her, maybe she'd been made to forget her, too, in which case he didn't want to bring her up anymore than he wanted to bring his dinner up.

They had a very strained conversation that really did proceed pretty much exactly the same as the last one, but was made literally more palatable by the addition of a very nice steak. Wally had just gone through the "Tell me about this project you're working on" part of the conversation, while very carefully avoiding the topic of Great-Grandpa Knight, when he heard a sudden ruckus from the lobby. One word made him twist around in his chair: "Flooding!"

Ariane! he thought. *Something's gone wrong!*

A hotel employee, the girl at the desk Wally had spoken to when he first came in, appeared in the entrance to the dining room. "Excuse me," she called in her lovely Scottish accent, "is Jessica Knight in...ach, there you are." She hurried over. "I'm terribly sorry, ma'am," she said in a low voice, "but there's been a plumbing malfunction in your room. None of your personal items have been damaged, but I'm verra much afraid we'll have to move you."

"Oh, dear," Wally's Mom said. She glanced at the waiter, but the desk clerk waved him away.

"Your meal is on the house," she said. "Management's compliments by way of apology for the inconvenience."

"How sweet," Mom said. She stood up. "We'd better get up there, Wally."

"I'll be right up, Mom," Wally said. "I need to go to the bathroom."

Mom hesitated. "All right," she said. "Don't disappear on me."

Wally didn't say anything, because, once again, he didn't want to lie to his mom – but he'd just seen Ariane appear in the lobby, waving frantically at him.

No chance of a doggy bag now. He grabbed the last two buns left in the breadbasket and ran to her.

CHAPTER TEN

GRANDMA'S BOOK

FLISH STARED AT ARIANE. Ariane stared at Flish.

"So you didn't melt away in the water like the Wicked Witch of the West after all," Flish said. "Dammit."

"That's cold, even for you," Ariane said. "Since that would have meant your brother melting away, too."

Flish laughed. "Don't try that. Rex told me Wally would have been fine."

"He did, did he?" Ariane said. "Same as 'Rex' promised to send help for him on that path on Cacibajagua, but really left him to die?"

"He didn't..." Flish began, but Ariane could hear the doubt in her voice, and remembered Wally had told her the same thing at the Castle.

"Yes, he did," Ariane said. "Flish...Felicia...I don't know why you hated me on sight, but don't let that blind you to the fact Rex Major couldn't care less what happens to Wally. He wants the shards, and he'd like to have an heir of Arthur to wield the sword once it's put back together, but that's all you are to him – a tool, a means to an end, like Wally was before. Wally wised up to what he's really like, and now he'd be happy to see Wally dead. If he ever decides you're no use to him anymore, he won't care any more about what happens to you."

Flish's fists clenched. "Shut up. I won't listen to your lies."

"You know you can't stop me from leaving this room."

"Because of your magic?" Flish sneered. "How'd that work out for you at the castle?"

Ariane frowned, suddenly wondering if Flish had a point.

"What I want to know is why you're in this room to begin with." Flish's eyes flicked to the coffee table. "Wait...that's that book of family stories my Grandma Knight wrote. The one that has the story about great-grandfather Knight's 'treasure'..." Her eyes widened. "It's not the Holy Grail, it's the hilt of Excalibur! Rex was *right*. There *is* a family connection!"

And with that, Ariane decided their little *tête-à-tête* had gone on long enough. Though she was still woefully low on energy, she had enough to reach for the nearest water...

...the toilet tank.

She couldn't see it, off to Flish's right in the bathroom, but she didn't need to. Maybe she couldn't use the shards to transport Flish against her will, but to her relief, Flish's mere presence wasn't enough to stop her using her other powers. The water exploded out of the top of the tank, carrying the lid with it. Both lid and water smashed into the wall behind Flish, who yelped and spun around – giving Ariane an opening to grab Grandma's book and run past her, not into the hall, but into the bathroom.

"Give that –"

Back, Flish's shouted sentence presumably ended, but Ariane had already plunged her hand into the toilet bowl and vanished.

She popped up an instant later in the fountain pool in

the village square, stumbled out, ordered the water off herself and the book, and ran for the Claymore Arms. She pounded up the steps and into the lobby just as hotel employees charged up the stairs, presumably to deal with the flood she'd just caused on the third floor.

Wally was in the dining room, standing at a table with his mom. Ariane waved frantically at him. His mom turned and, not paying the slightest attention to Ariane, hurried for the stairs.

Wally hurried over to Ariane instead. He held out both hands, a bun in each one. "Best I could do," he panted.

Ariane took one bun, put the book in Wally's freed hand, and then took the other bun. "I had to take it," she said. "Flish was there and figured out I was after it."

"Flish!" Wally stared up the stairs. "Mom didn't say anything about her. I'll bet Major told her to forget her, too."

"Told who to forget who? And what do you mean, too?"

"I'll explain later." He turned to face her again. "Let's just get out of here."

They ran out into the dark street, and across to the alley from which they had first observed the inn's entrance. In its darkness, they stopped. "If Rex Major suspects there's some kind of link to Great-Grandpa, too, we pretty much just proved it by taking the book," Wally pointed out.

"Flish made that connection anyway," Ariane said. "At least she didn't see inside the book. Not that there's much there." She quickly told Wally what she'd read.

"He'd already hidden the treasure away but someday he'd be with it again," Wally said slowly. "It's almost like a riddle."

"Maybe he intended to retrieve it at some point, but he died first," Ariane suggested.

"Maybe," Wally said. "But maybe he meant exactly what he said. Maybe, in the end, he did go to it!" He stared at her, eyes wide and white in the semi-darkness. "Maybe he buried it where he already knew *he* was going to be buried!"

Ariane felt a chill. "You mean...you think it's in his grave? We have to go *dig up his grave?*"

"Maybe not," Wally said hastily, but Ariane was pretty sure he was only saying that because he'd guessed from the sudden squeak in her voice just how freaked out she was by that idea. "Maybe it's just somewhere close by. In the church, maybe."

"God, I hope so," Ariane said. She shuddered. She'd always hated horror movies, and especially those scenes – and every horror movie seemed to have one – where the heroes had to dig up a grave and opened the coffin to reveal a mouldering corpse grinning at them, with rotting skin hanging from its bones and worms climbing in and out of its...

"Hey!" Wally said, touching her arm with his hand. She jerked and the horrible image vanished. "It's just a guess."

Unfortunately, Ariane thought, *it's a darn good one.* She closed her eyes for a minute. "All right," she said. "All right." Her eyelids flicked open again. "But we can't go there right away, even if we are in yet another race with Rex Major. I don't have the energy, Wally. I really, *really* need sleep. Real sleep, not drugged sleep." She remembered she was holding the bread he'd brought her; she raised first one hand and then the other to her mouth and practically inhaled the two buns. "Caffeine and carbs won't do it this time," she mumbled through a full mouth.

Wally looked back at the inn. "We can't go back in there. And we can't check into another hotel. I'm pretty sure an under-aged couple trying to get a room together would raise eyebrows. And possibly bring the cops."

"I don't need a room," Ariane said weakly. "Just some-place with a roof."

Wally thought. "Can you get us back to that loch near Castle MacPhaiden?"

Ariane sighed. "I think so. But we can't knock on the door and ask for Alex again."

"No," Wally said, "but we know we can get into that little tunnel in the walls, the one for the postern gate. It's not very big, but at least it's sheltered. And nobody's likely to stumble over us there."

Ariane nodded wearily. "All right," she said. She looked up – the skies were still cloudy. She took Wally's hand. "Here goes."

The jump was short, the fatigue enormous. And after they emerged from the loch, they still had to find their way, in near-total darkness, up to the castle. If not for the lights still blazing on the castle's exterior, it would have been impossible. Ariane wondered if those lights were still on because Alex was searching for them. She hoped not. Surely by now Wally's mom had talked to him and told him she'd seen Wally at the Claymore Arms – and that Wally had vanished again.

Ariane sighed, feeling sorry for Wally, for Wally's mom, for Alex, and more than a little for herself. She'd never been more tired, and the moment they slipped into the tunnel beneath the walls, she slumped down with her back against the rough stone and closed her eyes. She felt Wally sit down next to her, felt the warmth of his body next to hers, but it barely registered before she was fast asleep.

She woke an indeterminate time later sore and stiff and hungry, leaning on Wally as he leaned on her. Looking around at the cold, dank tunnel, she couldn't believe she'd slept there all night without waking, but from the grey light seeping in from both ends, clearly she had.

Wally was *still* asleep, leaning on her shoulder, mouth open a little, breathing heavily. She gazed fondly down at him. She'd thought him a homely, geeky, annoying kid when they'd met. But so much had happened since then, even though it had only been a few months, that now she couldn't imagine being without him.

She wished they could maybe just go for poutine or a movie sometime, go on an ordinary everyday teenager date, instead of flying through the clouds or scrambling through caves or popping up in random pools or...

...or digging up graves.

She shuddered. She couldn't help it. The motion brought Wally awake. "What...?" He sat up, blinking.

"You're drooling," Ariane said helpfully.

"What...?" Wally repeated. He wiped the back of his hand across his mouth. "Oh. Sorry. Gross."

Ariane grinned. "Don't mention it. Sleep well?"

He groaned. "Barely at all. It was already getting light before I dozed off." He yawned and stretched and scratched. "But what about you? It's way more important that you slept well than I did!"

"I did all right," Ariane said. "Exhaustion is better than any sleeping pill ever invented. Knocked me out as fast as Rex Major's tranquilizer, but without the side-effects."

"Does that mean you can take us back to Saskatchewan?"

"Yes," Ariane said. "But not straight to Cannington Manor."

"Why not?"

"Because I don't know exactly where it is," Ariane said. "I'll need a map." She stretched, and found sore places where she hadn't even known she had places. "Ow. We should start bringing an air mattress with us."

"Bit bulky in the backpack," Wally pointed out.

"Worth it," Ariane said. Her stomach growled, and she sighed. "Also, I'm hungry."

"Again?" Wally said in mock surprise. "You had a nutritious meal of dinner rolls not six hours ago."

"Not again," Ariane corrected. "Still." She considered. "Actually, *always*, at least when I'm using my power this much."

"There must be something in the village," Wally said.

Ariane nodded. "Mom and I found a coffee shop on Mother's Day. Let's head there."

They scrambled out of the tunnel beneath the castle wall and, with the bulk of the wall and cliff hiding them from any any prying eyes in the castle, headed toward the road...

...only to see, far down the valley, the van belonging to Jessica Knight's production company – and her rented car.

Wally stopped. "Clachgorm instead, maybe?" he said hurriedly.

"Clachgorm it is," Ariane said. She grabbed his hand and took them up into the clouds.

A few minutes later they casually clambered out of the same pool around the ornamental fountain from which they'd departed the night before. A short reconnaissance turned up a picturesque tea shop. It was hard to believe, as she ate a couple of lovely Scottish scones, that just the morning before she and Wally had been having coffee in the good old Human Bean back in Regina.

Yesterday afternoon, here, she thought, remembering the time difference. *It's only just past midnight in Saskatchewan.*

She wondered how her mother and Emma and Wally's Aunt Phyllis were bearing up. They had to be terribly worried, but they also had to know that Ariane and Wally couldn't necessarily come home every night. Phyllis at least seemed to grasp that; sometimes Ariane thought Mom didn't, even yet.

But at least, now that she had had both rest and food, she could once more feel, deep inside her, the shining thread of power that linked her to her mother – the thread she had relied on to not only draw her to her mother's side when Rex Major threatened her, but which had taught her she could travel much faster...and do more with her power...than she'd ever dreamed.

Her mother had been able to feel that link, too, and though she could not send any kind of message over it, she took some comfort in thinking that, as long as that link remained, her mom at least knew she was alive.

Given the circumstances, that was the best they could hope for.

"So where do we find a map in Clachgorm, Scotland, showing you where Cannington Manor is?" Wally said. He'd gone thoroughly British and ordered kippers for breakfast. Fish for breakfast was not something Ariane was brave enough to face, especially fish that still looked so much like a fish, so she'd stuck to her usual bread products.

"There's no rush, is there?" Ariane said, as she took up her third scone and started to butter it. "It's the middle of the night in Saskatchewan."

Wally sipped his tea, then set it down again. "Well," he said. "Except..." he let his voice trail off.

"Except what?" Ariane said, already thinking she was probably going to dread the answer.

"Except," said Wally, "can you think of a better time to go grave-robbing?"

Ariane groaned. "Are we really going to do that?" she said weakly. "Dig up your great-grandfather's grave?"

"Only if we have to. But maybe the hilt isn't really in his grave, it's just somewhere nearby, in the churchyard or somewhere else in Cannington Manor. Maybe if we just go there, we'll be close enough for you to sense it and grab it, and then Bob's your uncle."

"I don't have an Uncle Bob," Ariane said, deadpan.

Wally blinked. "Um, that's just an –" She let a hint of smile through, and he laughed. "Got me."

She put down the second half of her third scone. It didn't seem as appetizing anymore. "We're going to need tools. And a flashlight."

Wally nodded. "Guess we're stuck here until the shops open. I think I'll have some more tea…"

Fortunately, "until the shops open," or at least the small hardware store they were most interested in, proved to be only another hour and a half. They had the last of the money Wally had stolen from Rex Major, converted into pounds sterling before they'd taken their Mother's Day excursion. They went in and bought two spades and a pickaxe, plus a flashlight apiece. On the theory – bolstered by considerable evidence – that Ariane would be starving again once they got to Saskatchewan, they also bought salt-and-vinegar "crisps," thick bars of chocolate, and four bottles of sugary lemonade.

By then the town library had opened, too, and a quick Google on the public computer terminals showed Ariane how to find Cannington Manor – and also revealed, as Wally had suspected but hadn't been absolutely certain about, that the park wouldn't open until the Victoria Day weekend. All Saints Anglican Church, beautifully restored just a few years before, was still used for services – but only on the second and fourth Sundays of June and July.

All of which meant Cannington Manor was most likely to be completely deserted – well, even more likely than it was to be completely deserted anyway at 2:30 in the morning, which seemed the likely time they'd arrive.

That didn't mean they'd be safe from detection,

though. "It's a provincial park," Wally said. "There must be some kind of security. The buildings will have motion sensors in them for sure, but we shouldn't need to go inside. There could be cameras scattered around, although I don't know who would be monitoring them, and it would take a long time for the Mounties to get there from Carlyle even if someone saw us. Still, we should show as little light as possible."

"While we try to find a grave and possibly dig it up," Ariane said. "Oh, that sounds easy."

Wally flushed. "I know it's not much of a plan, but have you got a better one?" he snarled. Then he blinked, and said, "Oh. Sorry."

"Sword?" Ariane said.

"Sword," Wally confirmed.

Ariane nodded her understanding and carried on as if he hadn't snapped at her. "No, of course I don't have a better plan. But grave-digging…"

"I know," Wally said. "I know. But…" He let his voice trail off in turn.

They walked silently through the streets of Clachgorm until they found a secluded park. Screened from any passersby by a thick hedgerow, they took each other's hands and leaped into the sky.

◄◄ ►►

Rex Major got the call from Felicia just after the pilot of his private jet told him over the intercom that they were about to begin their final descent into Toronto. "Did you get the book?" he asked without preamble.

"No," Felicia said. She sounded angry. "That bitch Ariane was there. She grabbed it and just about killed me… again."

Damn it, Major thought. *She's alive. And that means*

she still has both of her shards. "Just about killed you how?"

"With the cover of a toilet tank," Felicia said. "Just missed my head."

Major chuckled despite himself.

"It wasn't funny!" Felicia snapped.

"Of course not," Major said soothingly. "It's just that, 'death by toilet-tank cover' isn't a phrase you think of very often."

"Ha ha ha," Felicia growled.

Major's momentary amusement flickered away. "So she has the book," he mused. "That means she and Wally know whatever it has to tell them – and clearly they think it might tell them what I had hoped it might tell *us*. Perhaps your mother…"

"I asked her," Felicia said. "She doesn't remember anything that hints where Great-Grandpa's 'treasure' might be hidden. And she's very upset right now because Wally joined her for dinner and then disappeared again. She's worried about him."

"Leave that to me," Major said. "Is there another copy of the book?"

To his surprise, it was Felicia's turn to chuckle. "Not a print copy," she said. "But Mom had it digitized. And if you look at your email right about now…"

A familiar chime sounded from Major's computer. He opened the email, and grinned fiercely. "Forgive my earlier doubts, Felicia Knight," he said. "You have more than re-deemed yourself for your little shopping spree. In fact, I'll treat you to something special in that regard once you're back in Toronto." His smile faded. "Which now needs to be as soon as possible. I'll make the arrangements. "

"Mom's expecting me to stay around now that you made me go back to her," Felicia pointed out.

"Leave that to me, too," Major said. He was already

scanning through 'Grandma's Book'...and there it was, the hint he'd been looking for. It didn't say exactly where the treasure – the hilt of Excalibur, he was *sure* of it – had been hidden, but it provided enough information to get them close. And once he was close, he was sure he could find it, especially once he had retrieved his own two shards...

...and had Felicia Knight with him so he could draw on their power.

"Will we be staying in Toronto for a while once I'm back?" Felicia asked, clearly hoping that was the case.

"I'm afraid not," Major said. He read the passage in Grandma Knight's memoirs again. "We're going on a sightseeing trip – to Cannington Manor Provincial Park."

"Cannington Manor?" Felicia said. He heard dismay in her voice. "You're dragging me back to Saskatchewan?"

"Look at the bright side, Felicia," Major said. He folded down his laptop's screen, buckled his seatbelt, and gripped the arms of the chair tightly, his preferred position for every aircraft landing he had ever been unfortunate enough to experience. He closed his eyes. "If all goes well, it will be for the very, very last time."

"Good," said Felicia. "Good."

Major didn't respond; he was far too busy worrying about plummeting from the sky to a fiery death.

CHAPTER ELEVEN

GRAVE ROBBERS

Of all the places their quest for the shards of Excalibur had taken them, a dark graveyard in the small hours of the morning was close to the top of the list of Ariane's least favourite. It didn't make the very *top* of the list only because that spot was permanently reserved for the cave in southern France, where she had crawled for what seemed endless hours through blackness, certain she would be lost forever in its stygian depths...

She shuddered. Although she gave herself bonus points for the use of the word "stygian." *It pays to increase your word power,* she thought.

The blackness of the All Saints Anglican Church grave-yard at Cannington Manor was not *quite* stygian. There were a few lights in the park, and more in the farms not far away. Nevertheless, they did nothing to light the grave-yard itself.

Finding a place to materialize hadn't been a problem. There were a number of small sloughs surrounding the single street of old buildings and remnants of founda-tions that made up Cannington Manor Provincial Park. Better yet, the one they had chosen hadn't appeared to be frequented by cows – always a plus in Ariane's mind.

They had climbed out and crossed the "street" – just a gravel path – to get to the churchyard. In the dark, Ariane couldn't tell how many graves it contained, but after they'd crept through it, flashing their lights – dimmed by holding their fingers over them – at gravestone after gravestone, while her imagination insisted on conjuring up images of skeletal hands bursting from the ground to seize their ankles, she began to think it might be endless.

Except, suddenly, they found what they were looking for.

It was far from the oldest grave in the cemetery – many dated back to the very early days of the 20th century, and some to the latter years of the 19th. It had a plain granite headstone. In the dim red light that their finger-blocked flashlights produced, Ariane first saw an elaborate carved cross at the bottom of the grave marker. At the top of the headstone was a name, *EBENEZER ALEXANDER KNIGHT*. Below that was carved *1868–1951*, and below the dates, in smaller letters, the phrase *FAITHFUL UNTO DEATH*.

"Great-Grandpa," Wally said. He flashed the light to either side. To the right of the grave was a second one, with a headstone labeled *LAURA UMSTATTD KNIGHT, 1872–1957*. "And Great-Grandma."

He lit up Ebenezer's grave again. No bump or depression distinguished it. Nor had anyone put flowers on it, at least not in a very long time, unlike some of the other more recent graves they had seen. "Are we really going to do this?" Ariane whispered. Butterflies churned in her stomach.

"Do you feel anything from the hilt?" Wally said. "Because I don't."

Ariane closed her eyes – not that it made much difference in the dark – and concentrated. "No," she said. "But maybe…"

She turned off her flashlight and put it on the ground, pulled up her shirt, the night air cool on her skin, and unwound the tensor bandage from around her middle to release the two shards of Excalibur she carried. They seemed quiescent, completely uninterested in whatever they were doing or where they were doing it. She held the ancient pieces of steel out to Wally, one in each hand. He took them.

That certainly woke the shards up – she could feel them purring like a couple of kittens, so pleased were they to be touched by an heir of Arthur – but she still couldn't sense the hilt's location. It could have been under their feet or on the moon, for all she could tell.

"Well?" Wally demanded, still holding onto the shards.

She shook her head, then realized he probably couldn't see it, and said, "Nothing."

Taking the shards back, and feeling their disappointment as she did so, she returned them to their place beneath the tensor bandage. She let her shirt fall back down, though she didn't bother to tuck it in, and bent over to pick up her flashlight. Covering the end with her fingers again, she turned it on to shine a dim glow on Wally as he put his own flashlight on the ground, its butt against the headstone, so that it cast a long, low fan of light across the surface of his great-grandfather's grave, the nighttime dew on the long blades of spring grass sparkling diamond-like in the beam. He turned to the tools they'd lugged with them from grave to grave during their slow examination of the cemetery, picked up a spade, and held it out to Ariane.

Ariane hesitated, taking a long look around. Her eyes were dazzled a bit by Wally's unshielded beam, even though it wasn't shining in her eyes, but she thought that maybe, just maybe, it wasn't quite as dark as it had been. Surely that was the horizon she was seeing, and hadn't the stars been brighter a few minutes ago?

Sunrise was still a couple of hours away, because this

close to the solstice twilight was a long drawn-out affair, morning and night, but if they didn't dig fast, their cover of darkness would vanish.

"Well?" Wally said impatiently, still holding out the spade.

Ariane sighed, turned off her flashlight, returned it to her backpack, and accepted the spade. Then she looked down at Ebenezer Knight's grave, took a deep breath, and shoved the metal blade into the dirt. Wally's spade plunged into the soft ground a moment later.

They dug in silence, and Ariane quickly forgot about the creepiness of grave-robbing in the back-breaking realization that she'd never before done anything as physically hard as just digging with a shovel. They didn't have to dig up the whole grave – they just wanted a decent-sized hole down to the level of the coffin – but that was still a lot of dirt to move, and as the hole deepened they had to take turns getting down into it and tossing out the soil. Her back and arms felt on fire, the hole seemed to take forever to get any deeper, and all the while, slowly but surely, the light grew. At first she could only see Wally's face, glistening with sweat even though the air was cool, in the light of the flashlight he had put on the ground. But by the time they'd dug down two feet she could see him as a black figure, digging and swinging out the dirt, spade full by spade full, and then his face appeared as a paler patch, and then...

...almost before she knew it had happened, she could see everything. The sun wasn't up, and it was so early in the morning it would have been the middle of the night in December, but darkness no longer covered the prairie – and no longer hid them, if anyone happened to be looking.

And then, while Wally was taking a short break out of the hole, leaning against his great-grandfather's headstone, Ariane, the palms of her hands stinging from blisters, drove her spade into the ground for what felt like the millionth again...and hit something hard. She jumped back as though she'd gotten an electric shock, bumping into the side of the hole, now maybe a metre-and–a-half deep.

"It's gotta be the coffin," Wally said. He scrambled down into the hole next to Ariane, leaned over and scooped dirt away with his hands, and there it was, smooth, polished red wood, its grain darkened by long years in the soil.

"We're not opening it," Ariane said. "We can't open it, Wally. We *can't*."

Wally looked at her, his face pale in the pre-dawn light, his expression serious. "We may have to."

"We can't," Ariane said. "And not just because I don't want to," she added, although she absolutely did *not*. "We can't open it because it's getting light. We'd have to make this hole twice as big before we could even try to pry it open. And even that would only work if it has a split lid. What if it's one piece?"

"And you still can't feel anything?"

Ariane closed her eyes and concentrated once more on the shards. "Nothing."

"Maybe if you…touched the casket?"

Ariane grimaced, but it was only wood, after all – no matter what might be inside. She knelt down, her knees grinding in the loose dirt on the coffin lid, and pushed her hands against it. "No," she said. "Nothing." She looked up. "It may not be here at all, Wally," she said. "It may not even have been the hilt, or at least not the real one. This could be a wild-goose chase."

Wally shook his head stubbornly. "It all makes too much sense," he said. "Great-Grandpa's treasure *had* to be the hilt of Excalibur. And it's got to be close. He said he'd be with it again someday, and here he is."

"But here it's *not*," Ariane said.

Wally pressed his lips together. He'd been leaning down, hands on his knees, staring at the bit of exposed wood

Ariane had knelt to touch; now he straightened and turned toward the grave marker, his head and shoulders above the ground. His eyes widened. He stared at the grey stone.

"Hey!"

The shout came from somewhere far too close for comfort. Ariane spun in its direction to see someone – a caretaker, maybe, or a park employee, she couldn't tell, and didn't really care – running toward them from a picnic shelter not far away.

Wally was still staring at the tombstone.

"Wally!" Ariane cried. The sky was clear. There were no clouds to leap into. They'd have to get back to the slough. "We have to get out of here!"

Wally seemed to snap out of a trance. He blinked at Ariane, blinked across the cemetery at the man charging toward them. He'd almost reached the wire fence surrounding the graveyard, but he'd had to angle away from them, toward the gate on that side. "You kids stay put!" the man yelled.

But Wally was already scrambling out of the hole. Ariane struggled out after him, sod crumbling and falling back onto the coffin lid as she did so. Then they dashed in the opposite direction, toward the main gate by the church entrance and, more importantly, toward the pond beyond the gravel path.

"We left...the spades and pick..." Ariane panted as they ran.

"Don't need them anymore," Wally cried. He sounded remarkably happy for someone being chased by an angry man.

"Woof!"

Crap. And a dog!

The dog must have been off exploring on its own, but upon hearing the ruckus had clearly decided there were more interesting things to do than sniffing and peeing on trees, because here it came, racing down the street toward them – a mutt, a big one, and it didn't look friendly, probably because its master was still shouting angrily at them...

...and gaining on them, too, though not as fast as the dog. It would reach them before they reached the pond.

Ariane didn't have any choice. She reached out with her magic, drew a long shiny tendril of water from the pond, and flicked it at the dog like a whip. It hit with enough force to bowl the animal over. It yipped in shock, but was up again in a minute and twice as angry. It sped over the ground like a furred lightning bolt, but the delay had bought them just enough time. Even as the water-tendril splattered to the ground, Ariane and Wally's feet crunched through dry reeds and splashed into the edge of the pond – and an instant after that, they were gone.

They didn't go far. A couple of dozen kilometres west of Cannington Manor lay Moose Mountain Provincial Park, and if the nearby Moose Mountains would not have been called mountains anywhere other than Saskatchewan, they did have one thing in common with their far grander cousins to the west – lakes.

Wally and Ariane reappeared in a secluded cove on the shore of Kenosee Lake, and together they staggered out, Ariane drying them as they reached the shelter of the birch forest, just beginning to leaf out.

Panting, she plopped down on a log. She felt unreasonably angry, and she wasn't sure much, if any, of that anger was coming from the sword. Not this time.

"What a waste of time!" she snarled. "Two hours of digging for *what?*"

"I wouldn't call it a waste," Wally said. "At least we got some exercise."

Ariane suppressed the urge to lash him with a water-tentacle. "But we're no closer to the shard. And we were *seen.*"

"So what?" Wally said. "About the being seen, I mean. What he thinks he saw was so unbelievable he'll just come up with some other explanation that makes sense to him, even if it doesn't *really* make sense. And as far the shard goes..." He sat down beside Ariane on the log. "It's true we didn't need to dig that hole. I'm sorry about that. I feel like an idiot."

Ariane felt her anger slip away. It was hard to stay mad at Wally when he took on that puppy-dog look. Although she still thought he seemed an unreasonably happy puppy dog, very unlike the one that had wanted to tear their throats out a minute ago. "You couldn't know it was a wild-goose chase," she said. "It seemed like a solid lead."

"Oh, I didn't say it was a wild-goose chase," Wally said. "And it absolutely was a 'solid' lead. *Rock* solid." He grinned, that same old homely grin he'd always had. The one she loved.

Usually. This time, not so much. "What are you grinning about?" she said.

"Because I know where the hilt of Excalibur is," Wally said. "All we have to do is figure out how to get it."

◄◄ ►►

Rex Major sat in his office in his high-rise Toronto condo, researching Cannington Manor and not finding much of interest. It wasn't very large and it wasn't very old – historic in Saskatchewan terms, maybe, but certainly not in his. A century? Piffle. He'd literally *napped* longer than that.

But even as he scrolled rapidly through a rather dull description of the goings-on at the Beckton Brothers' big ranch house, Didsbury – *Arthur's knights could have taught these "bachelors" a thing or two about partying,* he thought – a chime sounded: an automated search he'd set up for news about Cannington Manor had just found something.

He opened a new tab. "Cemetery vandalized at Cannington Manor," read the headline on the CBC Regina site. He scanned it. "Two teens seen by caretaker...managed to elude capture...no vehicles, so may still be in the area...RCMP investigating..."

Wally and Ariane. It had to be. They'd read the same thing he'd read, in Grandma Knight's book, and interpreted it the same way he'd interpreted it – that Ebenezer Knight had hidden the hilt of Excalibur, passed down in his family for generations, somewhere near where he was buried, where he would "be with it again," as his daughter-in-law had recorded him saying.

But Wally and Ariane hadn't *found* the hilt. He knew that beyond a doubt, because he now had his two shards with him – he glanced at them, lying on his desk, two pitted lengths of ancient steel entirely out of place in the ultra-modern room. If Wally and Ariane had had the hilt, these two shards would be gone, flown to join the reunited three.

He fingered the ruby stud in his right ear. *So they guessed wrong. It's not in Ebenezer Knight's grave. The question is, can I guess right?*

He glanced at the time. Felicia was winging her way to Toronto on one of his company jets. She'd be landing at Pearson International in four hours. They could board his private jet the moment she was there, and be in Regina in another three. Cannington Manor was more than an hour's drive from Regina, so call it eight hours in total. Late afternoon in Saskatchewan by the time they got to the cemetery, but there'd still be hours of light left.

He realized he was still fingering the ruby. He released it, and let his gaze slide from the screen and across the two shards to rest on the black case containing the tranquilizer pistol. He had two more of the highly useful devices, a handy belt holster for each, and lots of darts. He'd arm a couple of likely employees with the other pistols and Command them to come along. If Ariane and Wally showed up – and based on past experience, they almost certainly would – they would be dealt with. In fact, that would be ideal – knock them out and put them on ice somewhere and he could take his time looking for the hilt. If it was buried anywhere in the graveyard, he could simply use the power the shards gave him, with Felicia's help to enable him to draw on it, to ask the earth itself what was buried in it. A small chest, somewhere close to Knight's grave, would seem the most likely. With his shard-enhanced power, he could draw it to the surface without ever touching a shovel.

Once he had the hilt, Ariane's two shards would come to him, Excalibur would be reforged, and with it he would swing wide the door into Faerie. Then, with all his old magical powers restored, plus the additional potency from the sword, the plans he had so painstakingly put in place over the past two decades could be executed at last – generals and politicians, the whole *world*, his to Command.

His allies on the other side of the door would come to his aid as well. So what if he had been out of communication for a thousand Earth years? Time did not pass, or matter, the same way in Faerie. Those followers would still be loyal, and with the door open, they, too, would flock to his side.

Earth would bow down to him and, soon after, Faerie would fall, its mighty knights and even its magic no match for the war machines Earth was so very, very good at creating. The battles would be vicious but short, and then at last both worlds would be united, to flourish under the one ruler they should *always* have had, the true High King, the ideal of which Arthur, uniting the tiny squabbling kingdoms of Great Britain, had been but a pale shadow.

High King Merlin. Long live the King!

Just a few more hours.

He caught himself fingering that damned ruby stud again. He released it and started making phone calls.

CHAPTER TWELVE

EUREKA!

WALLY GRINNED AT ARIANE. Ariane stared at him as if he'd just sprouted an extra pair of ears. He patted his head just to be sure he hadn't, because after all, magic...

But he had only the usual complement of two ears, though they were of the rather sticking-out kind. So the astonished look must be because she didn't believe him.

Maybe if you explained? a rather sarcastic inner voice commented. *Instead of just going for the cheap drama?*

"I noticed it just before we had to run," he said.

"Noticed what?" Ariane demanded. She sounded exasperated, and he supposed he couldn't blame her.

"The hilt," he said. "It was in plain sight all the time. Well, kind of."

"Wally..." Ariane said. He heard a gurgling sound behind him, and glanced around to see the water in Kenosee Lake heaping itself up into a nastily bubbling hump.

Hastily, keeping an eye on the water, he said, "Did you get a good look at Great-Grandpa's headstone?"

"I guess."

The water subsided, and he turned to face her again. "Did you see that weird carved cross on it?"

"I saw a cross. Didn't think it was particularly weird. Lots of headstones have crosses."

"Not like that one. I didn't notice it when we first looked at it, because the light was so dim. But when I turned around in the hole in the morning light, it was right in front of me, and that's when I realized it's not a cross at all. Anyone would think it is, because it's on a headstone, but it's *not*." He let his grin spread to its widest. "It was a carving of a sword hilt, with a few centimetres of blade still attached."

He expected Ariane to shout "Eureka!", but instead she kept giving him that you've-got-extra-ears look. "So? Wally, a *carving* of a hilt doesn't do us any good. We need the *actual thing*. And it could be buried *anywhere* in that cemetery. Or not there at all. Someone might have found it while digging another grave. Some treasure-seeker could have turned it up. It still doesn't help."

"I disagree," Wally said, his grin slipping in a surge of irritation, only some of it from the sword. "I don't think it means the hilt was buried nearby. I think it means the hilt is right there...*inside the headstone*."

"Inside...?" Still no improvement in her "God, you're weird" look. "Wally, that headstone is solid stone."

"Is it?" Wally said. "What if it was just made to *look* solid? What if Great-Grandpa had it made special, out of two pieces of stone, with an opening inside it for the hilt?"

"Years before he died?"

"Why not? Lots of people buy their tombstones while they're alive, and just leave space for the dates. It would have been perfectly hidden, inside a grave marker and inside a warehouse somewhere, and he knew he'd 'be with it' again someday. Which he is."

"But if we were that close, why didn't we sense it?"

"I know why *you* wouldn't," Wally said. "It would be bone dry inside that headstone. With no water in contact with the hilt, you can't sense it. Just like you couldn't sense the shard in the salt water on Cacibajagua."

"But *you* were able to sense it there." Ariane still sounded a little peeved about that, Wally thought. "If the hilt is in the headstone, and you were staring straight at from less than a metre away, why didn't *you* sense it?"

"I don't know," Wally admitted. "But Great-Grandpa may have known a thing or two about hiding shards we don't. You know, through lore passed down to him through the family."

"So just after we got caught grave-robbing, you want us to go back and smash the headstone? Don't you think they'll be keeping a close watch on the cemetery for a day or two? And what are we going to use to smash solid stone with even if we *can* get back there without getting caught? We left our pick when we ran and they're not likely to leave it lying around waiting for us."

Wally's irritation suddenly roared into full-fledged anger. "You got a better idea, 'my Lady?'" he snapped. "Another lead you haven't told me about? A feeling? Hearing any singing? Or maybe you just want to go back to Barringer Farm and wait for Merlin to figure this out and grab the shard first!"

Sword talking, he suddenly realized. *Oh, crap.*

"Ariane," he began hurriedly, "I didn't –"

But Ariane had already leaped up from the fallen log, her face red. "Don't you dare mock me, Walter Knight! *I am the heir of the Lady of the Lake.* The sword is *mine* to retrieve and to use as I see fit. Just because you're the heir of King Arthur, don't think you have an automatic right to the sword. It's the Lady's sword. Your ancestor just used it – and lost it due to his own weakness!"

Wally never saw the tendril of water form. The first he knew of it was when it slammed into his back, throwing him over the log on which Ariane had been sitting, driving the wood into his diaphragm so hard his breath *whooshed* out. Spots dancing in his vision, he lay there, soaked in icy water, fighting to breathe, fighting even harder to force down the rage pouring into him from the sword, the urge to get up and teach the sorceress a lesson, show her who truly wielded Excalibur.

Ariane dropped on her knees beside him. "Wally!" she gasped out. "I'm sorry…"

She reached down.

Don't let her touch you! shouted the sword, but Wally pushed back hard. *She's my friend…my* girlfriend…*I love her…she loves me…*

She loves me.

Her hand touched his arm. The water sprayed off of him again. It didn't help him breathe, but it made him warmer. And then she put her hands on his shoulders and helped him roll over and sit up, and took his fingers in hers and helped him to his feet, and her touch made the last of the anger slide away.

"That," he said when at last he had air enough to form words, "was awful. Ariane, I'm so sorry. The sword…"

"The sword," she said. "I know. I can't believe I let it make me hurt you." She sounded shaky. "Wally. What happens when it's complete?"

Wally swallowed hard, and pulled her to him in a hug. She hugged him back. Again he was startled to find he was taller than her now. He pressed his cheek against the curve of her head, her hair soft against his skin, and whispered, "I fought back against the power just now with the best antidote to anger I know, and it worked."

"What?" Ariane said. "What antidote?"

"Love," Wally said. He squeezed her even tighter. "Love."

⬅ ➡

"Love," Wally murmured, and Ariane thought her heart would break, though whether with joy or terror, she wasn't certain.

The rage that had roared up in her out of nowhere – no, not out of nowhere, out of the two pieces of Excalibur she wore against her skin – had frightened her. The sword was clearly agitated, angry, furious they had not yet found the hilt, turning them against each other not because it was sentient but because it was *not*: it was just raw emotion, raw desire, raw rage. *Kill your enemies* was its one thought, its one motivation, and it saw almost everyone as an enemy – even when its power was being felt by two individuals who were actually friends. *More* than friends.

Wally thought their love was strong enough to fight off the sword's fury. Maybe so. Maybe when it was whole that fury would be less wide-ranging. Maybe then it would truly submit to their will.

But what if Wally was wrong? What if, once the sword was united, it had its own agenda, its own goals, and her mantra – *I control the sword; it does not control me* – was proved nothing more than childish defiance?

What if the Lady had lied to them?

Wally had suggested that long ago, and she'd refused to listen. But now, as their quest neared its end, she wondered.

This is no time for doubt, she told herself staunchly, but another part of her disagreed.

This is the perfect *time for doubt,* it murmured.

Though she really didn't want to, she let go of Wally and stepped back. "So," she said, "assuming you're really onto something, how do we break into a gravestone? Water's not going to do it. Not even ice – it's not like those rocks in the cave on Cacibajagua. There's no opening into it."

"But what if we made one?" Wally said excitedly. "All we need is a crack. Heck, we didn't look closely – maybe it's already cracked. Force in water, freeze it, do it over and over…"

"Awfully slow," Ariane said. "But maybe."

"Or maybe we don't have to do it there at all," Wally said. "If we could pull it out of the ground, you could transport it somewhere else, and we could break it at our leisure. Back to Barringer Farm, even. There are tools in the barn."

"How much would something like that weigh?"

"A lot," Wally admitted. "But no more than me, and you transport me."

Ariane thought about it, staring out at the blue water of Kenosee Lake, mist rising from it into the dawn light. "It might work," she said. "But we won't take it to Barringer Farm."

"Why not?"

Ariane turned toward him. "Because I don't know what will happen if we do free the hilt," she said seriously. "Look what the shards we already have just made us do. We were almost at each other's throats. What if we can't control the sword when its whole again? What if it made me lash out at Mom, or Aunt Phyllis, or Emma? It's too dangerous. We have to go somewhere far away from everyone."

"But without tools?"

"As long as there are rocks around we can break it open," Ariane said. "Just pick it up and drop it on something hard. I'm thinking the mountains."

Wally nodded. "Makes sense." He looked at the lake. "So, let's get back there and –"

"Wally, we were caught less than half an hour ago digging up a grave," Ariane pointed out. "We've stirred up a hornet's nest. There are going to be Mounties there soon, if they're not there already. We can't show up in broad daylight and just kick over the gravestone."

"I know," Wally said. "But we can't stay away all day, either. What if Rex Major turns up?" He frowned at the lake. "Wait a minute...there was another pond, right down at the end of the park, past the church, near that old two-storey house. It had some trees and bushes around one end. What if you take us in there, and we keep an eye on things from cover until the coast is clear?" He grinned. "It'll be like a picnic, only with the added excitement of possibly getting caught by Mounties."

"Lying in the weeds beside a slough avoiding law enforcement," Ariane said. "You're such a romantic." She sighed. "But I suppose you're right. And as long as we're close to the water we can get away even if we are seen." Her stomach growled. "Can we at least get something to eat first?"

"I wouldn't have it any other way," Wally said. He looked around at the woods. "There's a hotel on this lake somewhere. Bet you there's a restaurant."

"Let's go find out," Ariane said. She held out her hand, Wally took it, and they walked into the water and melted away.

◄◄ ►►

Felicia, when she disembarked from the company jet, was not happy to be told the trip to Cannington Manor was happening right that minute. "I thought I'd at least get one day in Toronto to go shopping like you promised," she grumbled.

"I'm just putting it off for a few days," Major said. "This could be the end of the quest, Felicia. New shoes will wait."

"Not if they're the only pair left and they're on sale," Felicia pointed out, but she followed Major across the tarmac to his private jet, parked not far from the just-arrived corporate one, and climbed in. She immediately went to the lounge refrigerator for a Diet Coke and a bag of sour-cream-and-onion chips.

Major didn't go to his office: he helped himself to a large whisky and settled down in one of the lounge chairs – buckling himself in, of course – to enjoy it. The engines revved up, and he leaned back and closed his eyes. Unless they died in the next few minutes on takeoff, or the plane suffered a catastrophic mechanical failure en route, or they crashed on landing, the final piece of Excalibur might soon be his.

It was a moment to savour.

So of course Felicia Knight spoiled it.

"Wally and Ariane both told me something," she said. She sat across from him, likewise buckled in, but slouched down and with her arms folded across her chest. The can of Coke sat on the low table between them, the unopened bag of chips beside it. Today she wore tight red-leather pants and a matching jacket, beneath which was a black T-shirt, sequins spelling out "Superstar" across her chest. Shiny high-heeled black boots encased her feet. The outfit was only slightly less inappropriate than the cocktail dress she'd insisted on wearing to Castle MacPhaiden.

"I wouldn't put too much stock in anything *they* told you," Major said. "They are my sister's creatures, and they will say anything to obtain the final piece of Excalibur."

"And you're saying you wouldn't?" Felicia said.

Major sipped his whisky, then held it in both hands as the plane started to roll. "What's this all about?" *And couldn't it wait until we've either made it safely airborne or died in the attempt?*

"They both said that no one came to help Wally on Cacibajagua. They said you didn't send any one, that you wanted him to die – or at least didn't care if he did."

Tread carefully, Major thought. "First of all, Felicia, as

I just said, they will lie without a second thought if it helps them get the hilt of Excalibur. And second, Ariane simply got there first and spirited Wally away before the men from the resort reached the spot. They're just trying to turn you against me."

"That's not all Ariane told me," Felicia said. "She also said that tranquilizer you shot her with almost killed her –"

"As I told you, that was a risk –"

"– *and* she said," Felicia pushed on, "that if she had… dissolved, or whatever the hell she does, Wally would have dissolved, too. Wally would have *died*." Felicia's eyes suddenly locked on his, hard as diamonds. "Were you lying when you said he'd be safe?"

"I was not," Major said, calmly, and sincerely, and, of course, utterly falsely. "Felicia, your brother betrayed me and I hold no particular fondness for him, but I know *you* do, and so I would never hurt him, because I know that would hurt you."

They were accelerating. They'd be airborne in a minute. Rex Major's heart raced in anticipation of that. It had nothing to do with whether or not Felicia believed him.

Did it?

She can't stop me, he thought. *Even if she betrays me, too, she can't stop me.*

Felicia didn't respond. Arms still folded, she leaned back in her seat and closed her eyes as Rex Major's private jet roared into the cloudy skies above Toronto.

CHAPTER THIRTEEN

THE HILT

Two and a half hours after they'd arrived in Kenosee Lake, refortified once again with carbs and coffee, and with a picnic lunch packed for later in the day, Wally and Ariane returned to Cannington Manor. At the southeastern end of the road that defined the village rose one of the handful of still-standing buildings, a two-storey white house. North of it grew trees and bushes, and close to those, partially hidden by them at one end, was a slough – a different and somewhat larger pond than they'd materialized in before, though not far away from the first. Ariane brought them back into being behind the trees, and finessed their arrival so that they didn't send up a geyser of water as sometimes happened when she was in a hurry. They crawled through mud and reeds out of the pond and in among the saplings and bushes, and she ordered them dry as they peered across and down the road toward the churchyard, through the large gate, big enough to admit a vehicle, in the eastern corner of the wire fence.

They could just see Ebenezer's grave past the corner of the church. Wally had half-expected yellow crime-scene tape and a dozen police cars, but that was clearly a function of watching too many cop shows. If, in fact, the Mounties *had* been called, they were long gone. The only person in sight was the man who had chased them earlier that morning, filling in the hole they had dug.

"This may be easier than I thought," Wally said softly to Ariane. "If he leaves soon, the park will be deserted..."

It was a nice thought, but hopelessly naïve, he realized a few minutes later, as two white trucks drove into the park through the main gate down at the far end of the gravel path. Workers got out, and for the rest of the morning and afternoon, the park was, if not exactly a beehive of activity, at least too busy for Wally and Ariane to show themselves. The workers seemed to be there to un-cart and reposition artifacts in the buildings in preparation for the summer visitors, who would begin to arrive the coming weekend. Winter's winds and melting snows had left behind trash and untidy mounds of decaying leaves, so a general cleanup was also in progress. As a result, there was always someone in sight.

But the first thing all those workers did, before picking up a rake or lifting a box, was make a pilgrimage to the churchyard to see the vandalized grave of Ebenezer Knight. Wally felt guilty about digging up Great-Grandpa's grave for no good reason – but he reminded himself that if they hadn't, he might never have realized that the "cross" on the gravestone was really a sword hilt, and that the hilt was not buried at all, but inside the stone.

If it really was.

It has to be, he told himself staunchly, but in fact he knew it didn't have to be at all – that the hilt on the stone might have just been Great-Grandpa's own private joke, referencing the treasure he'd actually hidden somewhere else, where no one would ever find it.

He glanced at Ariane. She'd dozed off shortly after they'd arrived, and lay stretched out on the ground, her head pillowed on her arms, her black hair, hanging loose, hiding her face from him. Once again he felt a wave of affection for her – affection, and a fierce hope that this would be the end of it, that as soon as the coast was clear, they would grab the headstone, smash it open, get the hilt, take the other shards from Merlin and complete the Lady's quest – and maybe, after all that, just be Wally and Ariane, ordinary high school students looking forward to an ordinary life.

Huh, he thought, looking back down and across the road to the churchyard where the hilt might be waiting. *Now that I put that into words, it doesn't sound nearly as wonderful as I thought it would.*

The fact was, he'd enjoyed the adventure. He'd always dreamed of being given a magical quest, and here he was, on the verge of fulfilling one. Oh, sure, there had been awful moments, moments of terror and despair and sadness – but there had also been wonderful moments, moments of pure joy.

Moment of pure love, he thought, looking at Ariane again.

The truth was, he'd never felt more alive than he had during the quest for the shards of Excalibur. He'd never experienced anything so exciting. He'd never done anything that felt like it *mattered* as much as this.

He remembered an old song from the First World War he'd run across somewhere online – *How ya gonna keep 'em down on the farm after they've seen Paree?* the lyrics ran. How could he and Ariane go back to being ordinary when the past six months had been so extraordinary?

Well, first things first, he reminded himself. *First, you have to get the hilt. And for that to happen, you have to have guessed right about its location – and this park has to empty out for the night.*

Which was still hours away.

Wishing he'd brought a book, wishing he could emulate Ariane and fall asleep – but afraid to, because if anyone wandered over to their hiding place for any reason, *someone* had better be awake – he tried to make himself more comfortable on the hard ground. *At least it's not muddy,* he thought – Ariane had taken care of that when they'd first arrived, drying the spot where they'd be lying – but that didn't make it any more like a feather bed. In fact, she had probably made it harder.

Ironically, considering he'd just been thinking how much he'd miss the excitement of the quest once it was over, this was shaping up to be the most boring day ever.

But then, despite his determination to stay awake, despite the hardness of the ground, his body betrayed him. He'd been shorted on sleep for days, his internal clock was horribly confused from the trips back and forth across the Atlantic, and he'd spent the early hours of the morning in hard physical labour. Without his even realizing it, his eyelids closed, and he slept, and slept soundly.

He awoke with a start to the sound of a slamming car door.

He raised his head and blinked through the screen of bushes.

The sun had leaped across the sky. It was late afternoon now. The slamming door belonged to a black SUV...

...and getting out of it were Rex Major, two men he didn't recognize...

...and Flish.

◄◄ ►►

The flight from Toronto to Regina passed both very quickly and very, very slowly for Merlin – quickly because he kept himself busy with emails and spreadsheets and other business-related activities, slowly because he didn't know what Ariane and Wally were doing, and if they somehow got to the hilt first...

But the two shards he now wore in a special money-belt-like apparatus around his waist remained quiescent. Ariane clearly did not have the hilt. Which meant he still had time.

They landed, got into the waiting SUV with the two employees from the Regina office of Excalibur Computer Systems that he had Commanded into new roles as henchmen, and began the long drive to Cannington Manor. Felicia remained in surly-teenager mode, staring moodily out the window at the fields, many still covered with vast sheets of shallow water from the only recently melted snow. *Ariane won't have any trouble finding water to work with*, Major thought, looking out his window at the similarly soaked fields on his side of the SUV. But he smiled at the thought, because both he and his men were armed with tranquilizer guns, tucked away in holsters on their belts. One shot, and Ariane would be out of commission and unable to interfere. And the guns would be just as effective at dealing with Wally, safely removing him from contention without triggering Flish's apparently still-active little-brother-protection circuits.

Most likely, of course, Ariane wouldn't appear at all. She and Wally had clearly struck out in *their* attempt to retrieve the hilt.

He wasn't sure what to expect as they pulled up to the closed main gate of Cannington Manor Provincial Park. Would there still be police on the scene, investigating the vandalism? Dozens of park staff to deal with?

But in fact, everyone seemed to have left for the day except for a woman who came out of a building near the gate. She knocked on the driver's window as they rolled to a stop. "Open it," Major told his driver, who complied.

"I'm sorry, sir," the woman said. "The park is closed.

It doesn't open to visitors until the long weekend."

"You will open the gate for us," Major said to her from the back seat, in the voice of Command.

"Of course I will, sir," the woman promptly replied.

"Are you in radio communication with any park staff remaining?"

"Yes, sir."

"After you have let us in, radio them and tell them we are here to investigate the grave vandalism and they are to vacate the park immediately. They will return in the morning as usual."

"Yes, sir," the woman repeated.

"Now, please," Merlin said, and leaned back.

For the third time, "Yes, sir." The woman opened the gate; they rolled over a cattle guard onto the gravel path running the length of the remnants of the village, down past the grey-and-white church. As they drove slowly along the path, a couple of workers came out of a building on the right and got into a white pickup. They drove in the opposite direction, giving Rex Major's vehicle a curious glance as they rolled by.

Another white truck came toward them from the biggest building in the park other than the church, a two-storey whitewashed house at the far end of the road. It passed them just as they pulled up at the churchyard gate. Rex Major climbed out of the SUV along with his two men. Felicia, sighing heavily, got out last and slammed the door with more force than was strictly necessary.

The men weren't dressed like his usual security types back in Toronto – he'd wanted them inconspicuous, and told them to wear what they would for a weekend at home. As a result, one of them had on a Saskatchewan Roughriders jersey over blue jeans, while the other wore a red sweater and khaki pants.

Merlin took a deep breath of the prairie air, rich with

the smells of damp earth and decaying vegetation and fresh growth. He looked back down the path to the main gate. The second white truck was just pulling out. As he watched, the woman he had Commanded closed the gate, got into a car, and drove away. No one else was in sight.

They had Cannington Manor Provincial Park all to themselves.

But as he'd expected, there *was* water close at hand, several bodies of it, large and small. Ariane could literally pop out of any one of them at any minute. "You two," he said to his henchmen, "search for the girl and boy whose pictures I showed you. If you see either of them, tranquilize them."

"Yes, sir," said the guy in the football jersey. Major had heard his name but hadn't bothered to remember it. They drew their tranquilizer pistols and moved away from the truck in opposite directions.

Felicia had wandered across the path to the side opposite the church to read the plaque in front of a hole in the ground identifying it as the former location of the parsonage. "This way," Major called out to her impatiently.

She gave him a flat, unresponsive look, but followed him to the churchyard gate and through it, between trees on their right and the church on their left.

Major went at once to what was clearly the Ebenezer Knight grave, although he couldn't see the headstone – a tarp had been thrown over the grave, presumably to protect it from rain until it was properly filled in again, and the tarp obscured the marker. But then, he wasn't interested in the grave marker. In truth, he wasn't even particularly interested in the grave, except as a starting point for his real search.

He undid the bottom couple of buttons of his shirt and reached inside to draw from the "money-belt" the two shards of Excalibur he had claimed for himself. Felicia was looking around the cemetery, and further afield, at the handful of other buildings still standing in the little community. "So this is where Great-Grandpa Knight moved to from Scotland." She shook her head. "I'd go crazy out here. What did they do for fun?"

"Fun is overrated," Merlin said. "It's a good thing you didn't live in Arthur's time. The cellphone coverage was terrible." He held out the shards of Excalibur to her. "Touch them," he said. "I need their power so I can search the ground for the hilt. Ebenezer Knight must have buried it somewhere in this churchyard."

Felicia gazed around at the graves. "I can't sense anything."

"Neither can I," Merlin said impatiently. "That's why I need the power of the shards." He thrust them at her again.

"All right, all right. Don't get pushy." She took hold of the other ends of the bits of broken blade.

Instantly Merlin felt his own magic wax as the power of the shards flowed into him. It was still nothing compared to what it would be once the sword was intact and he used it to swing wide the door into Faerie, but it was more than enough for this task. He closed his eyes and silently spoke the True Name of the soil, Commanding it to reveal its contents.

The earth beneath them responded. In an instant, he knew the precise location of every body, every scattered bone, every worm and rock and lost penny and old horseshoe nail and piece of broken crockery within the churchyard...

...and also knew the hilt was not among them.

It has to be here, he thought. *It has to!*

He cast his net wider, through all of Cannington Manor, probing its underground secrets.

Nothing. Nothing but rocks and rubbish, bugs and burrows.

"Dammit!" He released the power. Felicia let go of her ends of the shards and stepped back.

"No luck?" she said.

"Obviously," Merlin snapped. *And I was so sure. As, obviously, was my sister's pet, or she and Wally wouldn't have been digging here.*

He knew the hilt was not buried in the grave they stood next to, where Ebenezer Knight's bones mouldered peacefully inside his coffin – or, come to think of it, where he *assumed* Knight's bones did. After all, he hadn't actually looked to see if this was the elder Knight's final resting place.

He reached down and pulled back the tarp, revealing the headstone.

Ebenezer Knight, yes, there was his name, date of birth, date of death, and below that, a stylized cross...

He blinked. *No. Not a cross.*

A carving of a sword hilt.

THE hilt, one he knew well, though he had not seen it for more than a millennium.

The hilt of Excalibur!

Wild surmise gripped him. He turned to Felicia. "Take the ends of the shards!" he commanded.

"Why? You just said –"

"Do it!" he snapped, so fiercely she flinched. Mouth set in an angry pout, she took the ends of the metal fragments again.

Power flowed back into him. This time he focussed it on the gravestone. *Break!* he Commanded the rock of which it was made. *Shatter!*

Unable to withstand his magic, the tombstone of Ebenezer Knight shuddered as though in the grip of a very localized earthquake – and broke apart in cloud of dust and a shower of rubble.

And there, peeking out from the chunks of granite,

was a flat box made of silvery metal, its lid marked with golden runes Merlin recognized at once as components of a hiding spell – and that was as much proof as anything else that here, indeed, lay the hilt of Excalibur, the final piece of Arthur's shattered sword.

Fierce elation surged through him. He let go of his ends of the shards, leaving them in Felicia's hands, and dropped to his knees. At last! *At long, long last –*

He reached for the box.

CHAPTER FOURTEEN

EXCALIBUR REFORGED

"ARIANE, WAKE UP!"

Ariane awoke, suddenly and uncomfortably – not just because she'd come straight out of a muddled unpleasant dream in which she had been floundering in an oil-slicked sea, trying desperately to keep her head above the filthy salt water, but also because she was, literally, uncomfortable. In fact, she felt as though she'd bruised bones she hadn't even known she had, sleeping on the ground.

"What –" she began, but Wally shushed her frantically.

"Major," he said, barely mouthing the words. "He's here. With Flish. And backup."

Ariane blinked. She raised her head and peered out through the screen of bushes.

Sure enough, there was a black SUV – just once, she wished Major would choose another form of transportation, like a red minivan or a blue pickup – and two men, one wearing a red sweater, the other a Riders jersey, walking away from the SUV in opposite directions along the gravel path. Each carried what looked like a pistol with an extra-long barrel. "Are those...?"

"Tranquilizer guns," Wally whispered. "He knows

how close it came to working last time."

"It did work," Ariane said. "You saved us." She shifted her gaze as Rex Major and Flish came into sight past the corner of the church. "They're headed to the grave."

"He'll find the shard in the headstone," Wally groaned.

"He won't be able to sense it any more than we could," Ariane said, and hoped that was true. "And the stone is covered with a tarp. He won't see the carving, so there's no reason for him to think of the headstone."

For a few minutes it looked as if her optimistic assessment would prove correct. Major reached inside his shirt and took out two lengths of dull metal – *the other two shards!* she thought, and felt a surge of anger that *he* had them instead of her, their rightful owner as heir of the Lady who had forged them. She tamped down the reaction – it largely came from her own shards, of course – and kept watching.

Not that there was anything much to see. Major held out his two shards to Felicia, who took the other ends. Ariane understood that perfectly – Flish, like Wally, was an heir of King Arthur, and only the heirs were able to convince the broken pieces of the sword to work together. Presumably that would change once the sword was re-forged and whole once more. What exactly Merlin could do with the power of the two shards, she didn't know. His powers were largely a mystery to her, although on Caciba-jagua Island he had called down lightning, almost killing Wally with it, so presumably he was doing something impressive that she just couldn't detect.

From her point of view, Major simply froze, and stayed that way for several minutes while the two men continued to patrol, now wandering off the road along the southeast and northwest sides of the churchyard. *Keep going,* she thought. *Keep going. Out of sight.*

There's a nice lake over that way. Maybe you could jump in it. If she had to act, she'd have to act quickly, and the farther away Major's henchmen were from her and Wally's hiding place, the less likely they could take her down with one of those blasted poison darts in time to stop her from doing – whatever it was she had to do.

She considered that. What *could* she do?

If Merlin actually got his hand on the hilt, it would all be over. She knew whoever had three could claim all five, and she wouldn't be able to stop it, which implied an instantaneous transfer of some kind. If Merlin got the whole sword, would she be left with even the power of the Lady she had been given before she had possessed any of the shards, or would that desert her, too?

She couldn't afford to find out. That meant if it looked as though Merlin was about to claim the shard, she had to be ready to stop him – and she could think of only one way to do that...

The first time she had created a water-woman, she had done so in a frantic effort to save her mother, who was being held hostage by Merlin's men. Ariane had fed off the powerful link she shared with her mother by virtue of their mutual connection to the Lady of the Lake. She hadn't known until then that she *could* do it. But in the past month, since the ice came off the slough at Barringer Farm, she'd practiced it, frightening the cows in the process. It took a lot of power – but Major wasn't the only one with two shards of Excalibur and an heir to Arthur close at hand.

She rolled over on her back, pulled up her shirt, took the shards out from under the bandage that held them in place, then rolled onto her side to face Wally. "Take hold," she whispered. "I have to be in position in case he gets lucky."

"In position...oh!" Wally's eyes widened. He nodded, and took the ends of the shards.

Power sang through Ariane. Sleeping on the hard ground – and before that in the dank tunnel beneath the walls of the castle – wasn't the same as sleeping in her nice warm bed back at Barringer Farm, but it had still done wonders to recharge her magical batteries. She wished she had time to eat the lunch Wally had packed, but even without it, she had the power she needed.

She poured her consciousness out of her body and into the water behind them, the slough in which they had materialized, and formed the water into a girl-shape around the seed of her mind, like an oyster covering a bit of grit with pearl. Girl-shaped, but not girl-sized. The water-woman towered two feet taller than Ariane herself.

She could see through the eyes of the water-woman as if she were looking through her own. She glanced down to see her physical body stretched out again as if asleep, and Wally staring up at her with wide eyes. She would have smiled at him if she had a face, but she hadn't bothered to waste any power on that level of detail. She raised her watery head to peer through the screen of trees, and saw that the two men were coming back toward the SUV now, while in the churchyard, Major still stood frozen…

…no. Suddenly he stirred. She saw him say something to Flish, though she couldn't hear the words. He stared around the churchyard. Then he looked down at the grave, reached out – and pulled the tarp off of the grave-stone.

He's seen the carving, she thought. *But will he make the same assumption Wally did?*

Apparently so.

Rex Major turned toward Felicia, and held out the shards again. She took them. He stiffened.

The gravestone of Ebenezer Knight shattered into a hundred pieces.

Ariane dared not wait any longer.

In the shape of a giant woman made of muddy water, she charged toward the churchyard.

◂◂ ▸▸

Wally stared up at the giant water version of Ariane. He'd seen her create watery figures before, but never one this large, this fierce looking. Practicing at the farm, she'd made them as real as possible, so that they looked exactly like her, clad in foam instead of clothing. They'd also been the same size as her. But this one...

This one was a monster, a giant, vaguely female form with no recognizable face at all, just a smooth egg-shaped head, glaring out over the park like a peregrine falcon looking for a gopher to devour. He turned to follow the thing's gaze. Major stood by the grave, unmoving – and then suddenly he reached down and pulled the tarp from the headstone. He stared at it, and Wally knew he'd seen the same thing he had – the "cross" was really the hilt of a sword. Major turned toward Flish, and held out the shards again. A moment's silence – and then, with a sound that rang out across the quiet churchyard like a gunshot, the granite shattered. Major released the shards and bent down to pick something up from the rubble...

And Ariane's water-woman tore through the screen of branches, which momentarily shredded it into a cloud of spray that instantly leaped back into its form as it hurtled across the road and dashed toward the churchyard faster than an Olympic sprinter.

Riderman and Sweaterman had just returned to the SUV. As the water-woman erupted into sight they spun toward it – and, not surprisingly, froze. Ariane's water form grew long tentacles that slapped the tranquilizer pistols from their hands. The weapons whirled away, one smashing into the side of the church, the other vanishing into a patch of weeds. Then she punched each of them in the chest, knocking them onto their backs. The shock seemed to break the Command that Merlin must have put on them – they scrambled to their feet, stared around wildly, and then ran for the SUV, the doors slamming even as Ariane's watery simulacrum splashed through the churchyard gate and briefly vanished from Wally's sight behind the church as she tore across the cemetery to Ebenezer Knight's grave – where Rex Major was even then pulling a rectangular box of silvery grey metal from the rubble of the grave marker.

Ariane's watery form reappeared, barreling down on Flish and Major. Flish looked around and Wally heard her scream as Ariane's water-woman knocked her aside like a running back bowling over a defender, sending her rolling across the ground. Merlin straightened sharply and spun to face the onrushing apparition, but Ariane's water-arm lashed out and the box holding the hilt flew away from him as the tranquilizer guns had from his henchmen. It bounced off the tree that grew against the southeastern fence. The water-woman knocked Merlin flat on his back on top of Ebenezer Knight's shattered tombstone.

That's my cue, Wally thought, and sprang up and dashed toward the churchyard at the same moment the SUV roared to life and took off, spraying gravel.

Merlin bellowed in anger, and tried to get up, but every time he moved Ariane slapped him down again. Wally ran through the big vehicle-sized gate in the churchyard fence's eastern corner, dashed to the box, grabbed it and ran back again toward the pond near which Ariane still lay in her trance, controlling the water-woman.

Something whizzed by him like an angry bee and buried itself in the ground ahead of him – a tranquilizer dart. Merlin wasn't completely helpless after all. Gulping, Wally redoubled his efforts, crashing through the brush to

Ariane's side and throwing himself down beside her. "I've got it!" he cried.

◄◄ ►►

Through the eyes of her pond-water golem, Ariane watched Wally run back toward the slough where her real body lay. She heard a *pfft!* and turned to see that the second she had turned away from him Major had regained his feet, drawn his tranquilizer pistol, and fired after the fleeing Wally. Furious, she swung a watery arm, but this time he ducked under it and scrambled on his hands and knees back across the ground to where his two shards of Excalibur lay, close to Flish, who was sitting up staring at the water-woman with wide, white eyes. Merlin grabbed the shards and thrust them at Wally's sister. "Take them!"

Kill your enemies, Ariane's own shards urged her. *Kill your enemies!*

She swung her massive liquid body around and took a step toward Merlin and Flish – but then Flish took hold of the shards.

A howling whirlwind sprang into being out of nowhere, ripping up grass and dirt and even bits of the broken headstone. It slammed into Ariane's liquid body, whipping it into spray that she tried and failed to pull back into shape. Just like that, the water-formed body was gone. Thrown back into her own body, she screamed from the shock of the sudden dissolution, and snapped open her eyes to find Wally kneeling beside her, holding out the flat box of silvery metal, inlaid with strange gold markings, that had been hidden inside Ebenezer Knight's gravestone.

"The hilt!" she gasped. She grabbed the box. "Give it to me!"

"I was going to," Wally said, voice almost angry, but she knew that surliness came from the shards, whose anger she could feel inside herself as well, and ignored it. She scrabbled at the box with fingers that seemed not to want to work.

The whirlwind that had blown apart her water body roared toward them from the churchyard, a miniature tornado, a funnel of dust and swirling leaves that would hit them in an instant. She crouched lower, sheltering the box, still trying to open it, as the whirlwind crossed the road and tore into the trees...

...and then, suddenly, her fingers found the two small catches, and lifted them, and the box popped open.

At long, long last, she beheld the final piece of the sword Excalibur, the culmination of their quest.

Fine gold wire wrapped around and around the ancient sword's hilt, from which protruded a few centimetres of pitted steel blade, with a jagged break at the end. The pommel, a heavy black disc, had a small hole in it.

Ariane took all that in in an instant, then seized the hilt and lifted it from its hiding place.

Power ran through her like an electric shock. There was a sharp pop, a miniature thunderclap, and where before there had been only two shards of Excalibur at her feet, there were suddenly four, as the two Merlin had stolen from her, the two they had so heartbreakingly lost, one in the south of France through Wally's misguided betrayal, one on Cacibajagua Island where Merlin had left Wally for dead, appeared out of thin air.

In the same instant, the approaching whirlwind simply *ended*, its burden of dust and leaves and twigs and gravel dropping to the ground just a few metres away. But even if it had kept coming, howling like a banshee, she wouldn't have heard it, because in that moment all she could hear was the sword.

She'd dreamed of this instant. She'd expected the song of the sword to finally be complete, the five pieces to join together in a symphony of joy, or satisfaction, or triumph, perhaps even gratitude – but there was no song. Instead, the sword *screamed*, howled a sound of pain and fury and frustration that made her drop the hilt and scramble back from it, hands over her ears, though that did not and could not block out the horrible noise of the angry blade, for the sound was inside her head, inside her soul, filling the world.

"Wally!" she gasped. "Take the hilt!" *If I can't make it sing as a whole, maybe the heir of Arthur...*

Wally didn't hesitate – he seized the hilt avidly, so eagerly Ariane knew he'd wanted to claim it from the moment he'd seen it, his own connection to the sword and his own inherited power urging him to wield it as he had been born to do.

The moment Wally's fingers closed around the gold wire, the shrieking cacophony in Ariane's head quieted, as it had in France when Wally had taken hold of the first two shards they'd recovered. Here at last was the glorious music she had hoped to hear, and even as Excalibur exulted, the shards began to glow, red, then orange, then bright yellow. Heat rose from them, so intense Ariane had to scramble back even farther. The broken piece of blade protruding from the hilt glowed as hotly as all the others, and Wally, not as though it burned him, but as though he were in a trance, responding to a command only he could hear, placed the hilt on the ground.

The moment he did so, the other pieces of the sword moved, sliding together, forming themselves into one long blade, a white-hot shaft of metal. As the sword reforged itself, it sang a single ringing chord of joy that brought tears to Ariane's eyes – and yet, it still wasn't quite as perfect as she had imagined or expected. Deep within that chord was a single sour note. The blade was complete, and yet something was still missing...

...something vital.

Excalibur seemed to recognize it. The sourness grew. The chord of joy blew apart in echoing discord that made Ariane gasp in pain.

And then came *rage*.

As white-hot as the blade it sprang from had been an instant before, anger and fury flooded out from Excalibur, pouring into Ariane, who leaped to her feet to face Wally, who had likewise scrambled up and now glared at her with murder in his eyes. "What did you do wrong?" he screamed at her. "You ruined it!"

"*I* ruined it?" she yelled back. "*You* were holding the hilt. What did you do wrong?

This isn't right, an inner voice, almost lost in the cacophony of the infuriated sword, tried to tell her. *It's not Wally's fault. It's not your fault. Something else is going on...*

"A very good try," said a voice she knew, a voice she hated, a voice that should have sounded defeated, but instead sounded triumphant. "A very good try, indeed. You almost won the game. No doubt you thought you had. But you really should have known better. You should have known I would have an ace up my sleeve."

Ariane spun toward that hated voice, all the rage she'd been feeling toward Wally suddenly directed to a new and far more deserving target.

Rex Major – Merlin – stood ten metres away, on the gravel path, wearing a sardonic smile.

Over his shoulder peered the white face of Wally's sister.

CHAPTER FIFTEEN

THE LADY RETURNS

EVEN AS HE REACHED for the box containing the hilt of Excalibur, Merlin heard the wheels of the SUV spinning on the gravel of the park road, but the sound might have come from a dream – it meant nothing to him. His hand gripped the box. He drew it from the rubble. He stood, and turned...

...and saw a giant liquid woman-shape rushing toward him like one of the long-dead giants of Faerie.

Cold, filthy water, stinking of rotting vegetation, slapped the box containing the hilt out of his hand, sent it sailing across the cemetery to bounce off the lone tree against the southeast fence. A second watery tentacle punched him in the chest, knocking him flat, the broken pieces of Ebenezer Knight's tombstone digging painfully into his back. He tried to scramble up, and was slapped down again...and then again...and then...

The onslaught stopped. The watery figure had turned its head to stare in the direction the box containing the hilt of Excalibur had been thrown. Merlin scrambled to his feet at last, saw Wally snatch up the box from the base of the tree and run toward the gate. Furious, Major pulled the tranquilizer pistol from its holster and fired at the boy.

It would have taken an extraordinary bit of luck to hit him at that distance, and it wasn't forthcoming. The shot went wide. The water-woman saw it and swung angrily back toward him. This time he was ready for her, though, and ducked under the lumbering liquid arm, throwing himself headlong toward where his shards of Excalibur had dropped, yelling at Felicia to hold them. He didn't know if she'd have the presence of mind to obey, but she scrambled forward, and together they seized the shards.

With the surge of power that roared through him at that touch, he conjured a whirlwind. The viciously swirling mass of air ripped the water-woman into fog and spray. As it disintegrated, he shouted, "Keep hold of one shard!" at Felicia. Drawing back the second one, he shoved it into his pocket, then turned and drove the whirlwind toward the bushes where Wally had run, and, with Felicia struggling to keep up at his side, holding the other end of the shard he still gripped in his left hand, he strode after it. If he could stop Wally and Ariane from drawing the hilt from the box, he might still...

...but even as his tame tornado ripped into the bushes behind which Wally and Ariane crouched, its winds died to nothing and it vanished.

In that same moment, so too did the shards of Excalibur he had gone to such great lengths to retrieve. One instant he and Flish were holding one and the other was a heavy weight in his right pocket, the next they were gone as though he had never had them.

With them went his power, leaving him with only the faint trickle that found its way to him through the almost-closed door into Faerie.

Light blazed on the far side of the bushes, the hot white light of metal heated almost to melting, and he knew the deed was done. Excalibur had been reforged. The great sword of King Arthur was whole once more...

...almost.

Merlin reached up to touch the ruby stud in his right ear. He'd hoped it wouldn't come to this – but it now had, and he could still win, and that was all that mattered.

He strode forward to break the bad news to the two teenagers he had every intention of murdering the moment the sword was his at last.

◄◄ ►►

Wally stared at Merlin, and at his sister standing behind the sorcerer, and even in that moment, face to face with their mortal enemy, his first thought was, *What on earth is she wearing?*

The little black cocktail dress on a cold rainy day at Castle MacPhaiden in the Scottish highlands had been inappropriate enough but, in Cannington Manor, this red-leather ensemble with the black boots really took the cake.

But then he tore his gaze away from her and focussed on Merlin, although it was hard to think clearly with the fury of the sword burning in his brain. Something was wrong with it, seriously wrong. It was complete, and yet *not* complete. Some vital component was missing.

"What are you talking about?" he said. "We've got the sword. You don't. You lost."

"Five shards of Excalibur," Merlin said. "That's what my sister told you. But there was a tiny detail she left out. Yes, there were five shards of Excalibur. But there were six *pieces*." He grinned, and Wally was reminded of a moment, back at Thunderhill Diamond Mine in the Northwest Territories, when Merlin had grinned just like that, and for a moment he had seen the death's head beneath the skin, the ancient sorcerer lurking beneath the veneer of the urbane modern businessman. Here it was again, a frightening glimpse into the reality of their antagonist, and for a moment, with the sword screaming in his brain, he despaired. *Why did we ever think we could succeed? We're just a couple of kids. He's* Merlin. *He's…*

But then anger rose up in him and burned away the despair. *And we've reforged Excalibur despite his best efforts to prevent it. Just two kids. With the power of the Lady of the Lake. And the blood of King Arthur.*

"You're lying," he snarled. "The sword is complete. The blade has remade itself. The *hilt* was the last piece."

"But you don't have the whole hilt." Merlin lifted his hand and touched his earlobe and suddenly, sickly, Wally understood. How often had he noted that ruby stud, that strangely barbaric piece of jewelry, so out of place on a businessman like Rex Major? He looked down at Excalibur.

At the hole in the black disk of the pommel.

"I see you begin to grasp the reality of your situation," Merlin said. "I have always had this one little piece of Excalibur, this one fragment that has kept the door into Faerie from closing, a tiny jewel through which a trickle of magic has continued to reach me down through the centuries, all during my long confinement and ever since I used it to free myself. And until the sword has this final piece in its hilt, it is not complete – and not fully yours."

"But we still have the sword, and all you have is a stupid piece of jewelry," Wally said. "Which looks ridiculous on a guy your age, by the way." He seized the hilt of Excalibur again and lifted it, ignoring the way it screamed angrily in his head, unfulfilled and furious. "We're not giving you the sword, and we know you can't take it from us by force."

Merlin's grin grew fiercer. "Can't I?"

"If you could, you would have already." Wally shot a glance at Ariane. Why wasn't she speaking up? Why was she so silent?

To his dismay, he saw that she had dropped to her knees and now sat back on her haunches, hands hanging loosely at her sides, head thrown back, eyes closed, face white.

"Oh, that was true enough when the sword was in *pieces*," Merlin said softly. "But now that it has been re-forged, it is true no longer. It is so close to being whole, that becoming whole is all that matters to it. It wants to be complete. It wants to be wielded."

'The Lady made it. It belongs to the Lady!" But the sword dragged at Wally's arm, as though it were made of lead, as though it wanted to free itself from his grip. "She forged it! It wants to be with her!"

"The Lady forged it, yes," Merlin said. "But we were... closer then. I did not have a hand in its forging, but I offered a gem to decorate the hilt, a magical gem, a link to me, so that I would always know where the sword was, where Arthur was. I could even communicate to him through it.

"But then my sister betrayed me – betrayed our family, Clade Avalon. We had ruled our clade side by side, and together had opened the door from Faerie to Earth, found Arthur, raised him up as High King, helped him unite Britain. We intended to use Britain as a beachhead to conquer all of Earth, to annex it to Faerie – a whole new world of possibilities for our stagnant and hide-bound race.

"But the other clades were jealous. Oh, they claimed they were against our project because they found it unethical, but really, they knew they did not have the knowledge or power to open a door to another world as Clade Avalon had. They feared our ascendancy. And of course the Queen opposed our efforts because eventually we would have overthrown her.

"She came to my sister, and offered her lands and power and, of course, sole control of Clade Avalon, if she deposed me, exiled me to Earth. I found out about the plot too late to stop my own imprisonment in an oak tree by the sorceress Viviane, but not too late to hold one piece of magic to myself.

"Knowing Arthur was doomed, knowing the Lady would reclaim Excalibur, I took the gem from the hilt and kept it. As long as that gem remained in my possession, Excalibur could not be taken from Earth, the door into Faerie could not be closed completely...and, as you have just discovered, Excalibur could not be reforged success-fully." He held out his hand. "You might as well give it to me, boy," he said softly. "Because if you do not, I will kill you with my bare hands."

Behind Merlin, Wally saw Felicia's eyes widen. "No!" she said.

Merlin's face contorted with anger. He spun, and the back of his hand cracked across the side of Felicia's face. She fell to the ground, crying out in shock and pain. Hand on her flaming cheek, she raised wide eyes to look up at the sorcerer.

"Quiet, brat!" Merlin snarled, glaring down at her.

Rage, born of fear and frustration, born of the sword, born of everything that had happened in the past few months, exploded up in Wally like gasoline poured on a fire. He dropped the useless sword and charged Merlin. "Don't touch my sister!" he screamed, and crashed into the sorcerer from behind.

Merlin stumbled forward and tripped over Felicia, who cried out again, then scrambled away on all fours. Wally jumped onto Merlin, trying to pin him, but the sorcerer, stronger and faster than Wally expected, rolled over and shoved Wally away so hard he literally flew through the air and thudded to the ground. Lying there, trying to get his breath, he saw Merlin scramble to his feet. "And now at last – at long, *long* last – I get to kill you, Wally Knight!" the sorcerer snarled. He strode toward Wally –

– and then froze, staring past him with widening eyes.

Wally twisted around to look.

Ariane had Excalibur. Both hands wrapped around the hilt, she was pointing it at the sky, her eyes wide and staring and strangely unfocussed in her pale face. "She's coming," she whispered. "The Lady is coming."

Wally looked up in the direction the sword pointed...

...and saw a hole opening in the blue vault of the cloudless Saskatchewan sky.

◀ ▶

Ariane barely heard Merlin's words, or Wally's replies – something about a jewel the sword needed, a jewel that Merlin, not the Lady, had made; Merlin had it in his ear.

She knew it was important, knew it was vital, to get that jewel, but she couldn't seem to focus on it amid the waxing cacophony of the sword, growing louder and louder and louder and louder, blotting out everything else. Lost in the screaming in her own head, she sat on her haunches, arms hanging loose at her sides, blind and deaf to everything else...

...and then, deep within the screaming, she heard a voice, a voice she'd heard only once before, months ago, but recognized instantly.

The voice of the Lady of the Lake.

"Take up Excalibur," the voice said, distant and faint and yet somehow clear as a bell even within the angry roar of the frustrated sword. "Lift it up, and the door into Faerie will open wide. The gem from the hilt is not necessary for that. Take up the sword!'

But Wally had just picked up the sword himself. She wanted to cry out to him, to order him to give it to her, but she couldn't speak, could hardly move. She gasped for air. She couldn't seem to draw enough into her lungs. She felt as if a vast weight were pressing down on her, crushing her.

Flish said something. Merlin spun and struck her across the face. Wally screamed, "Don't touch my sister!", dropped Excalibur, and charged Merlin. Ariane gathered all of her strength, broke the strange paralysis that had gripped her, and lunged for the sword.

Her hand closed around the hilt. The sword still screamed its frustration and incompleteness – but it also screamed with power, power that dwarfed everything she had drawn from it thus far, power that rocked her back on her knees again, gasping. "Open the door!" the Lady cried, her voice as strong and clear now as though she stood by Ariane's shoulder...and, somehow, Ariane knew how to do that, or the sword knew how to do it. In the end, it amounted to the same thing.

She lifted Excalibur, raised it to the sky, drew on its power – and opened the door into Faerie.

It began as a small dark spot in the middle of the clear afternoon sky, like a rip in a blue curtain, but it quickly grew. Boiling black clouds poured out of the doorway like a swarm of flies, swiftly covering the sky, blotting out the sun. The clouds spread down from the sky to the horizon in seconds, surrounding Cannington Manor and the fields around it in a wall of swirling darkness. Lightning tore across the zenith like a bright ragged rip in the clouds, and thunder hammered the earth.

The temperature dropped precipitously. Mist raced inward from the wall of clouds. In an instant, the world faded away, reduced to a circle maybe ten metres in diameter.

Merlin stood stock still, face unreadable, staring around him, waiting for something. Or someone.

And then, behind him, past the road, in the field southeast of the churchyard, mounted knights rode out of the mist, or faded into existence from it – it was hard to be certain. Ariane lowered the sword and stared at them.

There were twelve in all, riding snow-white steeds that

looked like horses until you saw the bony ridges on their foreheads and the sharp spurs on the heels of their clawed feet. Each knight's armour gleamed in the grey mist with its own eldritch light, sparkling green and blue and white and gold. Every suit was a work of art, a masterpiece that would have brought people from all over the world to see it had it been in an earthly museum. Each knight carried a naked sword, laid across his lap as he sat his steed, one hand on the hilt, the other on the reins.

Then, behind them, a thirteenth rider appeared. This one rode unarmoured and unarmed, for she was a woman, wearing a long flowing dress of silver, bound about the waist with a belt of diamonds. Diamonds and silver likewise adorned her hair. Ariane had never seen her in the flesh, but there could be no doubt that this was the same Lady who had appeared to her and Wally in the chamber beneath the surface of Wascana Lake as a living sculpture of water, the Lady who had set them on the quest to find the scattered shards of Excalibur before Merlin – the quest they had just completed, and yet also failed.

"Brother," said the Lady of the Lake to Merlin, who had turned to face her and her knights as they materialized from the mist. "We meet again at last."

"It *has* been a long time," Merlin said mildly. "I am sorry I have not had the opportunity to come home and see what you've done with the place. I was unavoidably detained."

"The blame does not lie with me," the Lady said. "Your choices had consequences, as all choices do."

"As will yours," Merlin said.

The Lady laughed, a sound like a mountain brook tumbling down a rocky slope. "Dear brother, do you *still* imagine that you can somehow reclaim Avalon and challenge the Queen? Even now, when my heir…" For the first time she looked at Ariane, and bowed her head, ever so slightly, in recognition, "…holds Excalibur whole?"

"Not *quite* whole," Merlin said.

"Ah, yes. The jewel with which you contaminated my perfect sword," the Lady said. "The jewel that prevented me from removing the sword from Earth, the jewel that has provided you your paltry portion of magic in all the years since. Did you really think you had kept secret from me the fact you held it still?"

You *kept it secret from* us, Ariane thought, but she held her tongue.

Wally scrambled over to her on his hands and knees. "Are you all right?" he whispered.

"Shh!" she hissed. "Listen." But though she kept one hand on the hilt of the sword, she reached out with the other and took his.

"It's true the jewel still prevents me from taking the sword back to Faerie," the Lady of the Lake said. "But there is nothing to prevent me from taking the jewel from *you*." Her face hardened. "I will have my knights seize you by force and cut your ear off – or your head – to get it if you do not give it up freely."

Lightning flashed again, somewhere high in the mist, and thunder rumbled. A cold wind sprang up, hissing in the reeds behind Ariane and Wally and in the nearby bushes. Light rain began to fall.

"And you think it will take a dozen Faerie knights to accomplish that?" Merlin said. He still sounded more amused than concerned. "I'm honoured."

The Lady shrugged. "I have never doubted your power, brother. Only your wisdom. You had only to accept the Queen's decree that Earth was to be abandoned to its own devices and the door between the worlds closed, and you could even now be ruling in Avalon at my side once more. Your ambition – and disobedience – are what brought about your downfall."

"And what are your plans for me now?" Merlin said.

"Am I to be taken back to Avalon in chains?"

The Lady's expression hardened. "You have been banished from Faerie, by order of the Queen," she said. "No. You will remain here."

"Without magic."

"You have wealth and power enough to live out your life in comfort," the Lady said. "And it will be a long life, too, far longer than that of an ordinary human, even without your magic. The Queen is merciful."

The rain pattered down. Merlin stared at his sister for a long moment. "I think you actually mean that to be comforting," he said at last.

"I am still your sister," the Lady said. "I still care about you."

Flish still stood beside Merlin, looking ridiculous in her red-leather outfit. The mark on her cheek where Merlin had struck her was almost the same colour. She glanced at Wally.

"I see you brought your best knights, too," Merlin said. "No doubt another indication of your warm feelings toward me." His gaze flicked to the warrior at the Lady's right hand. "Sir Koris," he said. "Once you were the most loyal of the Knights of Avalon. Have you remained loyal in all the years since last I spoke to you?"

Koris nodded. "Yes, Lord Merlin," he said.

Merlin sighed. He looked back at the Lady. "Very well," he said. "Clearly I am outnumbered. May I request that Sir Koris be the one who takes the jewel from me? I know him to be a man of honour."

The Lady inclined her head. "That is acceptable." She looked past Merlin at Ariane and Wally. "You have done well, children," she said warmly, and her voice reminded Ariane once again of her mother's voice, as it had when she first met the Lady beneath Wascana Lake. "Ariane, Sir Koris will bring the jewel to you. Place it into the hilt, then

give the sword to me. And this will all be over at last."
She glanced at the knight. "Sir Koris?"

Koris, his face like white stone beneath the raised visor
of his helm, lifted his sword in salute. He rode toward
Merlin...

...then spurred his horse and galloped right past the
sorcerer and straight at Wally and Ariane.

At the same instant, more knights appeared behind
those of the Lady, bursting from the mist at a full charge –
and attacked the Lady's escort.

Ariane only glimpsed that attack, saw the flash of
blades, heard the clang and clatter of steel on steel and the
angry screaming of the strange steeds, before she had to
deal with the charging Sir Koris. With no time to think,
she acted instead out of pure instinct. Water from the pond
behind them leaped up and formed into a lance made of
ice, which struck Sir Koris square in his metal-plated chest,
lifting him from his steed, tumbling him head over heels
over its haunches and strange scaly tail. He crashed face
down into the reeds and lay motionless.

Ariane leaped up, Excalibur still in her hand, while
Wally dashed forward and grabbed the knight's fallen
sword. Ariane ran to join him. "Now what?" he shouted.

Sudden as an upended bucket, the rain poured down, a
deluge now, whipped by wind that had risen to a howl.
Lightning flashed and thunder shattered the air in its wake.
The intensifying storm hid the battle among the knights of
Faerie, but Ariane could sense the Lady and Merlin's location, somewhere off to the west. Clearly the Lady had fled
and Merlin had pursued her, no doubt forcing Flish to ac-
company him. If they were going to somehow overpower
Merlin and take the jewel, they had to follow him.

*Finish the quest. Complete the sword. Get it into the
Lady's hand. Then this will all be over at last.*

"This way," Ariane said and, holding Excalibur, ran

toward the church, a dark shadow in the rain and mist that burst into vivid life every few seconds with another flash of lighting.

Shouts, the clash of weapons and the screaming of the strange steeds swirled all around them. Out of nowhere appeared a Faerie knight, whether one of the Lady's or one of the Merlin's Ariane couldn't tell. He struck savagely at Wally, but Wally, moving with dancer-like grace and speed, ducked under the blow and drove his own sword upward. It slid between two plates of the elaborate armour and into the back of the knight's knee, and he screamed and clutched at his leg, blood pouring from the wound, as his weird mount carried him off into the mist again.

Wally's eyes looked wide and frightened, but he flashed a grin at Ariane. "If only Ms. Mueller could see me now!"

Ms. Mueller? Oh, the fencing coach. Despite everything, Ariane laughed.

They reached the wide corner gate of the churchyard. The rain had cleared the earlier mist but was pouring down so hard visibility had scarcely improved. When lightning flashed again, gravestones stood out stark and white on the green grass for an instant before plunging back into wet gloom. Two knights battled on foot among the graves, their swords flickering as fast as the lightning, neither seeming to get the better of the other – but best avoided, Ariane thought, and besides, the Lady wasn't in the churchyard. She'd gone farther, and Ariane thought she knew where.

Ariane had made use of the smaller sloughs to the northeast of the townsite, but there was a much larger body of water to the southwest. She'd avoided that one because it was fenced, but a few strands of wire would hardly stop the Lady.

She altered course. Her inner sense of the Lady's presence grew stronger. Excalibur screamed ever more loudly in her head, a sure sign that not only the Lady but also that blasted jewel of Merlin's was close.

And then lightning flashed again and she saw them, brother and sister locked in their own battle, one fought without sword or shield or physical weapon of any kind.

The Lady stood with her feet in the water of the small lake, and behind her loomed a giant, a mass of water in human shape, but five times the height of a man. Merlin stood at the top of the slope leading down to the lake, hands outstretched, and in response to his silent magical Commands whirlwinds tore at that impossible figure, ripping spray from its surface, and lightning slammed down on it, exploding chunks of it into white-hot steam – but despite all the magic Merlin hurled at it, the giant held its shape.

Beside Merlin, Flish sat on the ground, knees to her chest, arms around her legs, head pressed downward.

Merlin had his back to Wally and Ariane. They would never have a better chance. Ariane tried to draw the rain into her own water-woman, but the near-hurricane wind blew it away before it could form.

Lightning flashed almost constantly now, and the sound of thunder was deafening, as bolts slammed home all around them, not just onto the water giant, but throughout the park. Ariane had to shout at Wally to be heard. "I'll hold Excalibur, protect it if anyone tries to come after it," she yelled. "You go after Merlin!"

Wally nodded grimly, and hefted the sword he had taken from Sir Koris, the fallen Faerie knight.

Ariane looked around. Not far away was a deep square hole in the ground, lined with concrete, all that remained of the flour mill that had once been Cannington Manor's pride and joy. "I'll take shelter in there," she yelled. She leaned over and kissed him. "Good luck!"

"You, too," Wally shouted back. He took one deep breath, then pelted off into the rain.

CHAPTER SIXTEEN

THE RUBY

THE GIANT RISING from the lake was the most terrifying thing Wally had ever seen – unless it was the lightning Merlin was calling down to fight it, bolt after bolt, their flashes leaving streaks of purple in his eyesight, their thunder making his ears ring and shaking him to his bones.

He wondered why Merlin didn't call lightning down on the Lady herself. *Maybe there's some magical law that prevents it,* he thought. *Or maybe he just really doesn't want to kill his sister, any more than she wants to kill him.*

Although that water giant was hardly what he'd call non-life-threatening.

His own sister crouched beside Merlin, curled up tight, and he ached to see her like that, ached when he thought of Merlin's hand smashing across her face.

As he recalled that, anger roared up in him again. He carried an ordinary sword – if any sword out of Faerie was truly ordinary – not Excalibur, but Excalibur was all but whole, and not far away, and it still fed his rage – not that his rage needed much feeding in that moment, as he raced toward Merlin, remembering everything the sorceror had done to them, to Flish, to Ariane, to Aunt

Phyllis, to Ariane's mom.

Kill your enemies, Excalibur all but shouted in his mind.

He had never killed anyone before, but there was a first time for everything. He lifted the sword...

A downward blast of wind smashed him to the ground like a giant fist. His stolen blade flew out of his hand and tumbled out of reach down the slope. Merlin didn't even turn around. "You're a fool, boy," he shouted above the tumult, as his hands wove strange patterns in the air and lightning continued to slash at the water giant. "Now lie quiet until I can deal with you properly."

"The Lady...will squash you...like a bug..." Wally gasped out.

"My *sister* is a one-trick pony," Merlin said. "Her giant is taking too long to form, and my men are winning the battle with her knights. They will join me shortly, and this will end – for my sister, for Ariane, for *you*. Now! Be! *Quiet!*"

Suddenly it felt as if the air had turned solid around his chest, had become bands of steel that compressed, squeezing the breath from him. His vision greyed. His eyes bugged. He felt his mouth opening and closing like that of a landed fish, and to as little effect. He could not breathe...could not...

"Stop hurting my brother!" Flish screamed, and sprang from the ground like a cat leaping at a bird, all claws and teeth. She landed on Merlin's back and clung there, legs around his waist, arms around his neck, squeezing as hard as she could. He staggered, roaring what had to be oaths, though Wally could not understand them.

The invisible bands around Wally's chest loosened. He could breathe again. He tried to yell a warning to Flish, to tell her to run before Merlin struck her down.

But then she did the last thing he would ever have

imagined her doing, the last thing he would ever have believed her *capable* of doing:

She bit off Merlin's ear!

Not all of it, just the earlobe holding the jewel. Her white teeth flashed, Merlin screamed, and then Flish threw herself free of him, thudding to the ground, blood on her lips. She spat into her hand the piece of Merlin's flesh and the precious ruby jewel from the hilt of Excalibur, and scrambled toward Wally, holding it out, a gory trophy.

Merlin, roaring in pain and fury, turned quick as a snake and grabbed her ankle, but her outstretched hand was already within Wally's reach. He seized the bloody scrap, leaped up and ran back toward the old basement where Ariane waited.

Lightning struck the ground directly in front of him. The concussion threw him backward, blinded and deafened, but he kept his fist tight on the scrap of Merlin's ear and the jewel. He supposed Merlin was afraid of what lightning would do to the jewel, or he would have struck him directly. But now off to his left, from the direction of the churchyard, he could see four knights running toward them both, victors of the battle.

He didn't think they were the Lady's men.

He rolled over and got to his feet and staggered a few more steps past the smoking crater in the ground left by the lightning. He was almost to the basement. He could see Ariane, staring out at him over the concrete walls. Her mouth was moving, she was clearly shouting at him, but his ears felt stuffed with cotton after the thunder blast of the lightning bolt. He couldn't hear her – but it looked as if she was saying...

The rain redoubled in strength, and suddenly he understood.

Even as the knights closed the distance, he reared back

and threw the bloody piece of Merlin's ear as hard as he could.

◀◀ ▶▶

Ariane jumped into the basement of the old flour mill, Excalibur in hand, and looked out through the screen of weeds growing along the edge of the pit at Wally, who was racing toward Merlin, sword raised. "Wally!" she screamed as wind smashed him to the ground. She tried again to do something, anything, with the water in the air, but Merlin's control of the winds had negated all her power. With the door into Faerie open, he once more had full, or almost full, control of the magic he had once utilized in the service of Arthur, and those powers were far greater than she and Wally had ever guessed.

Even the Lady of the Lake was no match for him. At the same time as he contemptuously smashed Wally to the ground, a vast chasm opened at the feet of the Lady's water giant, just as it stepped forward at last to strike him down, and it drained away, losing coherence, falling as a massive waterfall deep into the Earth, a waterfall that seemed to carry with it all the Lady's strength, for she swayed, and then dropped to her knees in the mud at the very edge of that gaping hole, into which all the remaining water of the small lake from which she had formed her giant likewise poured. Fifty metres of fencing dangled over the hole, clumps of earth clinging to the feet of the wooden posts.

Ariane wondered briefly how the farmer would explain the damage to his insurance company, but the thought flitted through and out of her mind like an insect. She saw Wally struggling to breathe, and tensed, ready to spring up and run to his rescue, futile though it would be. Even now, four of Merlin's men were racing toward them from the direction of the church, and with her own powers over water rendered useless, they would strike her down and take Excalibur before she could even –

Flish leaped, strangled, bit, fell. Merlin screamed, clutching his hand to the side of his head, blood pouring through his fingers, then lunged after her, grabbing her booted foot. But Wally had the ear, and the ruby stud. He tried to scramble up and run.

Ariane cried out as lightning struck the ground between her and Wally, but the bolt vanished and he was still there, on his back, but already scrambling to his feet again. He staggered toward her, but the knights were almost on top of them, he'd never make it to her in time…

But though she could not form a water-woman, she could still make some use of the water in the air, and suddenly she knew what to do. "Throw it!" she screamed at him. "Throw it!"

Wally looked puzzled. He couldn't hear her! She shouted again, and whether at last her voice penetrated the howl of the wind, the rumble of thunder, Merlin's shouts, Flish's shrieks, and the pounding clatter of the approaching, running knights, or whether he read her lips, or whether he just trusted her…

He threw the bloody scrap of flesh, and Ariane formed the water into a long, thin lasso that seized it and pulled it back to her, fast as a striking snake.

"Kill them both!" Merlin screamed. "The girl first!"

The knights changed direction, angling away from Wally and running straight toward the flour mill basement. But Wally was still closer, and scrambled into the basement just ahead of them. Even as he did so Ariane, heedless of the blood and the "Ick!" factor, ripped the ruby from the tattered remnant of Merlin's earlobe, and placed it in the hole in the pommel of Excalibur.

The ruby glowed, red as fire, red as wine, red as blood,

as it settled into the hilt. And as it did so, at long last, at long, *long* last, the song of the sword rang out full-throated, pure and whole. A wave of fierce joy over-whelmed Ariane. She shouted, a wordless cry of pure pleasure and happiness.

The Faerie knights leaped down into the basement, raised their swords...

...and Wally seized Excalibur from Ariane's hand and met them head on.

◂◾ ◾▸

Wally felt the sword's shout of fulfillment, echoed by Ariane, as the missing jewel at last settled into its place – and also felt the sword's sudden keen awareness of impending bat-tle. Without even thinking about it, he seized Excalibur from Ariane and turned to meet the advancing knights.

Wally had had less than two years of fencing training, and he hadn't been the best on the team by a long shot. The knights of Faerie must have had centuries – millennia, even – to hone their skills.

But with Excalibur in his hand, none of that mattered. His opponents seemed to move in slow motion. He knew what they were doing almost before they did it, could dodge every blow, could judge exactly where he needed to be, and where his blade needed to be, to parry, and then to strike. In what felt to him like leisurely fashion, he cut the knights down, killing none of them – though the sword wanted him to, it *was* fully under his control, despite what Wally and Ariane had often feared, and it let him choose the blows that would incapacitate and cripple but not kill. Still, the quantity of blood that splattered him and his foes and Ariane and the blade would have made the scene R-rated in a movie, he thought with a strangely detached part of his mind.

The "battle" was over almost before it began. The knights lay moaning around the basement. Wally took a deep breath, and moved either by some impulse from the sword or from memories of Aslan's advice to Peter in *The Lion, the Witch, and the Wardrobe*, wiped the blade clean 'of blood on his shirttail.

"You still haven't won," snarled a hated voice, and Wally looked up to see Merlin standing at the edge of the basement, Felicia held tight against him, his left arm around her neck – and the point of a dagger at her throat.

◀◀ ▶▶

Merlin had moved far beyond mere anger to incandescent murderous rage, burning inside him hot and bright as the lightning he hurled all around him, exploding trees, shattering buildings. Most of Cannington Manor was ablaze now, burning despite the rain. Only the church stood unscathed, for he was bound by an ancient oath he had made to the Christians, when Arthur ascended the throne of England, not to harm their holy sites.

He dared not bring his lightning down on the two brats while they had the sword, and he had used all his earth magic swallowing his sister's water giant. The earth would object to being called upon again, and he *really* didn't want the land to be angry at him.

His torn ear burned, but he ignored the pain. He would heal the wound with magic when all this was over, and it would be as though it had never happened. It did irk him to think of how the blood had ruined his suit, but he supposed the rain and wind and mud and everything else had damaged it beyond repair anyway.

That was a minor annoyance. The major annoyance, the insufferable annoyance, the thing that fed oxygen to the raging fire of his fury, was the stubborn refusal of

Ariane Forsythe and Wally Knight to give up, to give him what he wanted – what he *needed*. What he *deserved*. They were nothing, nobodies, teenagers, *children*, and yet they had thwarted him at every step. If not for the fact the shards could not be taken from Ariane by force until the sword was reforged, if not for the fact that killing her before all the pieces were found would have shattered the power of the sword, she would have died long since.

For one brief moment he had had his chance. With Excalibur complete but for the jewel – *his* jewel – the sword, angry at being still unfulfilled, would have let him take it from Ariane by force. But that fool Koris had failed him in the same moment he had so wonderfully *not* failed him. All those years – not as many years in Faerie as it had been on Earth, since time moved differently in the two worlds, but years enough – Koris had remained faithful to Merlin, had cultivated others who remained faithful, and when the Lady had called on him to lead the expedition to Earth to retrieve the sword, had clearly arranged for the surprise attack that had thrown the Lady's plans into such chaos.

And yet he had *failed* to seize the sword, and somehow, while Merlin had been pursuing his sister, Ariane and Wally had slipped past the battling knights to be in just the wrong place at the wrong time – *again!*

And Felicia – he squeezed the brat harder. Heir of Arthur or not, she was clearly made of the same inferior metal as her brother. Neither could serve him. Neither was *worthy* of serving him, of leading his armies. He would kill them both and carry on alone, as he had fully intended to do before the dark day he had learned of Wally Knight's existence and heritage.

Wally was soft. Felicia was soft. He'd assumed they had shattered their filial bonds long since, as he had shattered his with the Lady of the Lake, as Arthur had shattered his with his half-sister, Morgause, mother of his bastard son

Mordred, who had slain him in the end at Camlann. But far from it – Felicia had actually *chosen* her little brother, chosen him over everything he, Merlin, had offered her and could offer her.

More fool she. Let her pay the price. Let Wally pay the price.

"Give me Excalibur, or I will cut your sister's throat while you watch," he snarled at Wally.

He knew the sword's power. He knew Wally, carrying Excalibur, was the equal or better of any swordsman who had ever lived in either world. The crippled knights moaning in the old basement were proof enough of that. But not even Arthur himself would have been able to reach Merlin before he drove his dagger into the girl's throat.

He saw the same realization cross Wally's face, and knew he had won. Wally Knight would give him Excalibur to spare his sister, as Ariane had once given him the first shard to spare Wally. And once Merlin had Excalibur, no one could touch him. Wally's surrender would be futile, of course. No one would leave Cannington Manor alive except for Rex Major. On the morrow, his conquest of Earth and Faerie would begin in earnest, and then...

Something struck him from behind, so fierce a blow it felt like his skull had exploded. He found himself on his hands and knees. He'd dropped his dagger. Felicia had escaped. What...?

Something struck him another stunning blow, this time in the ribs. He rolled over and over across the ground and ended up on his back, gasping for breath, staring up at a woman made of water...

No, not a woman. A girl.

Ariane.

CHAPTER SEVENTEEN

THE LADY AND THE LADY

NOT AGAIN, Ariane thought, as Merlin seized Flish and threatened her with his dagger. *Not again!*

She did not have Excalibur in her hand, but she didn't need it. Wally had it, and the power flowing into him was flowing into her, too, through the link between them – the powerful link of love she had discovered there after he had pulled her from the brink of dissolution during their near-disastrous journey from Scotland, after Merlin's tranquilizer dart had found her. It didn't matter which of them had the sword. It served them both.

It served them, they did not serve it.

Merlin's winds had died, but the rain continued to pour down, and with the power of the sword coursing through her, she closed her eyes and formed a water-body for herself, a perfect replica made of rain. The Lady of the Lake herself still knelt at the edge of the pit into which her water giant had collapsed, but Ariane's power had never felt greater. She looked out through the eyes of her water-body. Merlin was focussed on Wally, on Excalibur. He never turned around.

She froze the end of the water-woman's right hand into

a fist of ice, and smashed it against the side of Rex Major's head.

Stunned, he dropped the knife and Flish, who scrambled away from him, running to Wally's side. Wally took a step forward with Excalibur, eyes blazing, but Ariane shook both her head and the water-woman's, and he stopped.

Merlin was on his hands and knees. Ariane kicked him in the side with an icy foot, and he rolled across the ground, away from the basement. She strode after him. Her anger was boiling within her now, raging, and some of it was from herself, and some of it was from the sword. *Kill your enemies. Kill your enemies!*

Her watery right arm lengthened and hardened, and suddenly she held a replica of Excalibur, made of ice. She stood over Merlin, and put the frozen tip against his throat. He lay perfectly still, staring up at her. He didn't look frightened. He only looked furious.

She stared down at him. Hatred filled her. He had threatened her mother, her Aunt Phyllis, Wally. He'd almost killed her, and she knew if he had been the one with Excalibur at this moment, and she the one lying helpless at his feet, he would not have hesitated to drive the point of the sword through her throat and into the ground and walk away without a second thought as she choked to death on her own blood.

Kill your enemies.

I control the sword, the sword does not control me.

Kill your enemies. Kill him!

The icy blade trembled, but still she stayed her hand.

Wally joined her. He held the real Excalibur in his right hand, and his left arm held his sister around the waist. Ariane realized for the first time that he had not just grown taller than her in the months since all this had begun, he had grown taller than Flish.

"Ariane," Wally said. "Don't."

The water-woman could not speak, and Ariane dared not release her control over it to speak with her own mouth. She didn't move.

"Don't," Wally said again. "Please."

"Listen to the heir of Arthur," said a new voice, and Ariane turned the water-woman's head to see the Lady of the Lake approaching at last, her long silver gown bedraggled and mud-spattered, her hair tangled and full of wet leaves instead of silver mesh and glittering diamonds. She looked very much as Ariane's mother had looked on the night Ariane had found her on their doorstep after Mom's own encounter with the Lady, and Ariane took some grim satisfaction from that. "Let my brother live."

Ariane turned the water-woman's head toward Wally, then nodded at Merlin.

Wally understood at once. "I've got him," he said. He put the point of the real Excalibur close to Merlin's throat, and at last Ariane let the water-woman dissolve, the water washing over Merlin's face so he coughed and sputtered, and returned to her own body. She climbed out of the flour mill basement and stood to face the Lady.

"Why?" she demanded. "Why *shouldn't* I kill him after everything's he done?"

"Wally understands," the Lady said. She looked down at Merlin, whose eyes flicked from one to the other. "He is my brother. Despite all and everything, that is true."

"You intend to take Excalibur back to Faerie and exile him to Earth," Ariane said. "Where he will die. What difference does it make if he dies of old age fifty years from now or dies today?" She turned and looked down at Merlin, and she suddenly realized something else, something that added a bubble of terror to her still-boiling anger. "Wait," she said. "You told him that he would still be rich and powerful after you left. You don't just intend to leave him here, you intend to leave him here as *Rex Major*." She glanced at Wally, whose eyes narrowed, and at Flish, whose eyes widened. "He'll still be one of the richest men on the planet, and we'll be helpless." She glared at the Lady. "You intended to abandon us to his tender mercies – and he doesn't have any!"

The Lady's face grew stern. "It is not your place to question the ruling of the Queen of Faerie. She has decreed that he is not to be killed. I will exact a promise from him that –"

"No," Ariane said. "His promises are worthless. And how will you make him keep a promise once the door into Faerie is closed and you can no longer enter Earth?"

The Lady's expression darkened further. "You are my creation," she said dangerously. "You will do as I say."

"Your creation?' Ariane's anger blazed again, burning new fuel. "Creation? You said I was your heir."

"*Chosen* heir," the Lady said. "Not blood heir. I have no blood heirs on Earth. I am not human. You have my power because I chose to share it with you to accomplish my goals on Earth. You are a tool, and you have proved to be a very fine tool indeed. As a reward, before I close the door into Faerie, I will leave you treasure enough that you will never again want for anything. But that will be the end of it. My true power lies in Faerie, and you can never share in it, because you are merely human." She turned to Wally. "Your quest is at an end. Give me Excalibur, and I and all those who came with me will withdraw into Faerie. The door will close, and Earth will never again be troubled by magic."

Wally looked at her steadily for a long moment, and then, the point of the sword never wavering from Merlin's throat, turned his gaze to Ariane. "What do I do, my Lady?" he said, and for the first time, Ariane didn't object to him calling her that. In fact, she could have kissed him.

Later, she thought.

"Keep the sword," she said. She turned to the Lady. "You don't want us to kill Merlin? Fine. He can live. But he cannot remain Rex Major."

The Lady's eyes narrowed. "What do you propose?"

"You imprisoned him once," Ariane said. "For a millennium. Imprison him again. Restrain him so he can never again threaten us, or those we love. A century, two centuries, forever, I don't care."

A strange glow lit the Lady's face, and her eyes suddenly flicked past Ariane. Ariane glanced behind her to see the wounded knights Wally had bested in the battle in the basement vanishing, glowing bright and then disappearing into thin air as though they had simply evapourated. From all around Cannington Manor, similar glows brightened and faded – Faerie reclaiming its own, the wounded and the dead.

"I'm guessing that means you don't have a lot of time left here," Ariane said softly. "So what will it be? Imprison your brother, or watch him die?"

The Lady, glaring at her, took a deep breath. "Very well," she said. She walked over to Merlin and looked down at him.

"Don't do this," Merlin said. His eyes flicked from Wally to Ariane, then back to his sister. "You shared my vision, once. We were going to remake Faerie, rejuvenate our world with the resources of Earth. Arthur proved flawed, but our plan was sound. Join me again. We could still take this world, and then take Faerie. Together we could be King and Queen."

"It was a foolish dream," the Lady said. "These humans cannot be relied upon. As Arthur proved. As my own 'heir' has proved." She shot an icy look at Ariane. "If we ever let them into our world, they will be a cancer that will eat away at everything we have built there, until it becomes as befouled as their own. The Queen was right. The door between the worlds must be closed, and kept closed."

"Melina," Merlin said, his tone pleading, and Ariane blinked. *So that's the Lady's real name?* "Please." The last word was a whisper.

"Goodbye, Merlin," the Lady said. She put her hand on his forehead and closed her eyes.

"Noooooo!" Merlin shouted, a long, drawn-out howl that dwindled to nothing as his body began to glow, like the bodies of the knights. Unlike theirs, his body did not vanish. Instead, it *transformed*. Wally and Flish stumbled back as it lengthened, and twisted. It grew upright, but not like a man getting to his feet. Rather, it was as though his body were made of wax that melted and flowed into a new shape. The glow grew brighter and brighter until Ariane had to fling a hand over her eyes. For one brief moment it flared bright as the sun.

Then it went out.

Merlin had vanished. In his place stood a tree that had not been there moment before – an ancient, gnarled oak, taller than any other tree at Cannington Manor. In its twisted bole, if you looked at it just right, you could almost swear you saw the face of a man.

A very, very angry man.

"I have done as you asked," the Lady of the Lake said. She held out her hand to Wally. "Now, Excalibur."

"Wally," Ariane said. "Give *me* the sword."

The Lady's eyes narrowed dangerously as Wally, holding the sword flat in both hands, held it out to Ariane.

Ariane took it. The joy that filled its song, and her as her fingers closed around the spiraling gold wire of its hilt, took her breath away. She closed her eyes, and concentrated, letting that song rush through her, bearing with it all the magic of the sword, the magic keeping open the door into Faerie. She could feel, too, the strain on that door, Earth itself fighting to close it, like a human body trying to heal a wound, to seal it before infection could spread. It would be *easy* to slam that door shut, with so much pressure on it. All she had to do was withdraw the power keeping it open.

"You know," she said conversationally, holding up the sword and looking down its wet, shining length, "when you offered me your power, the main reason I accepted was because I thought there was a chance it might help me find my mother. Which it did. So thank you for that."

"Give me the sword," the Lady said. She sounded as though she were talking through clenched teeth.

"You played on that, of course," Ariane went on. "You talked about my mother when you 'recruited' me. You knew that would make me more likely to do what you wanted.

"And I *did* do what you wanted. I took the power. I set off on the quest. I thought I had to do it because, well, you're the Lady of the Lake and clearly you must be wise and good and wonderful and all-knowing. It was like when I was little, and I thought Mom was perfect in every way, and I should do what she told me because I wanted to be a good little girl.

"But Mom *wasn't* perfect. She ran off and left me. She thought she was doing it for me, but it was the wrong thing to do. It hurt me terribly. Then you came along, and I thought maybe you would be perfect in every way and I should do what you wanted me to because I wanted to be a good little girl.

"But you know what?" And now Ariane pointed the sword directly at the Lady. "You're not perfect, or wise, or good. You're an alien, an invader from another world. You and your brother came here a thousand years ago to try to set up Earth as your own private little kingdom, to make yourselves rich and powerful, like the Spaniards plundering South American gold. And so when you say you're going to close the door into Faerie forever, I don't believe you. I believe you'll be back, or others of your kind will. Earth isn't safe from you.

"So here's the thing." She lowered the sword. "I'm keeping Excalibur. *Wally* and I are keeping Excalibur. I'm keeping the power you gave me. And if anyone...*anyone*...from Faerie tries to come back to Earth and meddle in our affairs again, Wally and I will be waiting for them. And if we're dead and gone, then our *heirs* will be waiting for them. From now on, Earth is protected – by the power of Arthur and power of the Lady of the Lake – the new Arthur, and the new Lady of the Lake – and Excalibur."

The Lady's face had gone white while Ariane spoke, ice-white except for two red spots burning on her cheeks. "How *dare* you? *I* am the Lady of the Lake." She raised her hands, and the rain swirled and coalesced behind her, forming a water-woman twice her height. "Give me the sword or..."

Ariane and the sword laughed together. She reached out with her Excalibur-augmented power, and the Lady's water-woman dissolved into spray and fog. The Lady staggered as her own magic backlashed into her, like a snapping rubber band.

"You are *not* the Lady of the Lake," Ariane said. "*I* am. You are Melina of Avalon, and it's time you went back there."

She raised the sword again, as *she* had when the door into Faerie had opened – when she had opened the door, for it had come to her that that was exactly what she had done, that the Lady – Melina – had not opened the door from the other side, but had called to her to use the power of Excalibur to open it for her.

This time, she closed it.

Like water swirling down the drain, the clouds and rain surrounding them rushed into the sky. Twirling and spinning, black tatters of fog were sucked into the hole that had opened in the firmament above. Blue sky appeared all around the horizon, and swept upwards as the clouds departed, until all that was left was a small hole, an eye-hurting circle of ebony blackness at the zenith.

Melina reached out talon-like hands at Ariane, screaming, "I'll kill you for this, you little –"

Then she, too, vanished, her body flaring white before it was pulled up into the hole in a flash of lightning, lightning that leaped from where she had stood to that black hole high overhead...

...a hole that vanished as though it had never been.

A final deafening thunder-crack slammed down onto the prairie.

The late-afternoon sun shone down once more on Cannington Manor; on the smouldering, shattered remains of the historic buildings; on the litter of fallen trees and broken branches and scattered leaves; on the massive pit that had opened at the edge of the small lake, reducing it to a muddy depression; on the giant oak that had sprouted at the corner of the flour mill basement; and on All Saints Anglican Church, which alone shone as calm and undamaged as it had before the storm.

Ariane took a deep breath. "It's over," she said.

◀ ▶

Wally stared at Ariane as if he'd never seen her before. "Wow," he said. "That was...wow."

Ariane gave him a smile – just a small one, but definitely a smile. "Are you all right?"

He took his own deep breath. His side ached where Merlin had kicked him, and he thought he'd pulled a muscle fighting the knights, since the sword hadn't seemed to care that he wasn't a battle-hardened warrior and had made him perform moves his body had never even considered performing before and really hadn't appreciated having to perform now. But...

"Yeah," he said. "I'm all right."

He looked at Felicia, who had sat down on the ground, arms around her knees. "Flish...um, Felicia?" he said softly. "How are *you* doing?"

"I think I've got a loose tooth," Felicia said. "And I really could use some mouthwash. Merlin tasted terrible." She looked down at herself. "Also, what was I thinking, wearing this stupid outfit? Wet leather is the *worst*."

Wally stared at her, and then laughed. "I couldn't believe it when you did that," he said. "I mean...that was hard-core, Sis."

Felicia shrugged. "He would have killed you. I couldn't let that happen."

"Thank you," Ariane said.

Felicia looked up at her, studied her face for a moment, then looked down again. "You're welcome," she said. She didn't say anything else, but it was a start, Wally thought.

He looked around at the badly damaged park. "How are we going to explain all this?"

"We don't have to," Ariane said. "How about instead we all go home before anyone else shows up?"

"Go home?" Wally blinked at her. "You mean...I thought, I know what you said to the Lady, but I thought you must be bluffing. I thought with the door into Faerie closed, you'd lose your power." He studied her face. "In fact, I thought that was what you *wanted*," he added softly.

"That's what the Lady – *Melina* – wanted," Ariane said. "She wanted to use me to get the sword, then take it away and close the door and leave me here – *us* here – helpless, with her brother as rich and powerful as ever. She didn't care what happened to us after she had the sword. But you know what?" Ariane lifted Excalibur. It shone in the sun, and Wally was suddenly struck by its beauty. Its reforging had not only joined the pieces together, it had rejuvenated them – the blade looked brand-new. "The Lady's power over water never came from Faerie. It's from right here on Earth. And Excalibur is the key to accessing it." She lowered the sword and grinned at him again. "I have more power than I've *ever* had."

"And what will you do with it?" Felicia said unexpectedly. She stood up. "Become a superhero? Wear a cape? Get your own comic book?"

"Flish," Wally said warningly, but Ariane just laughed.

"Maybe that's not a bad idea," she said. "The superhero part. And maybe the comic book. Not the cape."

Wally blinked at her, and she laughed again.

"I don't know," she said. "I don't know what I'll do in the long term. But in the short term, I can tell you exactly what I'll do. This!" And then she strode forward and, to his complete and utter delight, kissed him, long and hard.

Felicia made a gagging noise, but he waved his hand at her to tell her to shut up.

Ariane pulled back, but then took his hand and squeezed. "And now," she said, "if you'll take your brother's other hand, Felicia…"

Felicia made a face, but she reached out and grasped it.

"Please keep your arms and legs inside the magic at all times," Ariane said, and Cannington Manor vanished from around them.

CHAPTER EIGHTEEN

FULL CIRCLE

ON AN EARLY MORNING in late summer, Ariane and Wally stood on the shore of Wascana Lake, looking out through the golden mist at the shadowy form of Willow Island, the very place where they had first encountered the Lady of the Lake ten months before.

Ariane carried a long case that had once held a fishing rod, with Excalibur hidden inside it. She could hear its song clearly – it purred like a kitten, contented to be whole, contented to be in the service of the Lady and the Heir of Arthur, though always wishing, just a little, that they would kill someone with it, just for old time's sake.

Not going to happen, Ariane thought.

They had passed a glorious summer. Ariane had taken them back to Barringer Farm, where her Mom and Emma and Aunt Phyllis had fussed over all three of them, bandaging what needed bandaging, listening to their stories of what had happened, and feeding them until they'd almost popped. Flish – Felicia, Ariane reminded herself again; she'd been trying very, very hard not to call Felicia by her hated nickname since their new rapprochement had begun so tentatively at Cannington Manor – had been quiet and withdrawn to begin with, but had thawed as the days went by, and by the time the real owners of Barringer Farm had returned she had seemed almost human.

They'd all watched the news coverage of the "freak storm" that had devastated Cannington Manor, the strange "pothole" that had swallowed the lake, and the mystery of the tree that had certainly never been there before but was there now, complete with a root system that delved half a dozen metres into the Earth. Nobody had come up with anything close to a believable explanation for *that*, but it was already bidding fair to become Cannington Manor's top attraction, and despite the damage to the old buildings, all now undergoing extensive restoration, the park had had more visitors that summer than ever before in its history.

Deepening the mystery was the fact that Cannington Manor had also been the last known whereabouts, just before the storm, of computer magnate Rex Major. Two employees of Excalibur Computer Systems had come forward to say they had driven him there, but that they had left him at his order and returned to Regina. They seemed confused about the details, but although they'd been questioned closely, in the end there was no evidence of foul play and they'd been released.

Authorities had eventually concluded that Rex Major had somehow perished in the storm, his body perhaps carried away by what was widely assumed to have been a tornado. A search of the area, however, had turned up nothing.

An alternative theory was that Rex Major had been involved in shady underworld dealings and had been murdered by the mob. A Toronto writer had gotten a quickie bestselling book out of that, and a TV movie, *Downfall of a King*, was already in the works.

With the return of Sam and Nancy Barringer to the

farm, they'd had to vacate, of course, but since Rex Major was no longer pursuing them, that had suited everyone just fine. Emma had returned to Estevan, and Aunt Phyllis, Ariane, Ariane's mom and Wally had all returned to Regina – where Pendragon the cat had shown remarkable indifference to their renewed presence in his life. Ariane, Wally and Felicia hadn't stayed long. Wally had phoned his mom and all three of them had headed off to Scotland to sightsee while Jessica Knight continued to shoot her "deeply personal" film about the strange history of her family. Alexander MacPhaiden had told her the family legend associated with the painting over his fireplace, and it seemed possible her film might actually come close to revealing the truth. Wally, Ariane, and Flish nodded wide-eyed as she told them her theories, but didn't offer any additional information. Fortunately, Rex Major's disappearance had not meant the disappearance of the funding he had arranged for the film.

Ariane had enjoyed seeing Wally and Felicia and Jessica Knight re-bonding as a family, and Wally's mom had been so happy to meet her and had made her feel so welcome that she hadn't felt like a third wheel – well, fourth wheel – at all. And during their four weeks in Scotland a few more things had been worked out, too.

Jessica Knight had taken the Knight house on Harrington Mews off the market, and had the furniture moved back into it from storage. She and Felicia and Wally would be living there, except when Jessica was away on long shoots. Felicia would be accompanying her – Jessica had officially hired her daughter as her assistant – and seemed thrilled by the opportunity.

Whenever they were away, it had been decided, Wally would stay with Aunt Phyllis and Emily Forsythe and Ariane, so that he and Ariane could continue their schooling. They were in the same grade now; Emma had determined that Ariane had, not surprisingly, made insufficient progress during the past year to advance to Grade 11, and so she was repeating Grade 10 as a classmate of Wally's.

She didn't mind.

In fact, she found she didn't mind much of anything. She'd never been happier.

The quest was over, the bad guy defeated, the sword of Excalibur whole once more...

...and she still had the power of the Lady of the Lake.

At first she'd thought she'd need to have the sword with her for her to draw on those powers, but in truth she could feel the sword wherever it was – which was what now brought them here to Wascana Lake.

"Are you sure about this?' Wally said. He glanced at her, his face shining in the morning light. He'd grown another two inches over the summer and he even had the beginnings of a mustache on his upper lip. He'd be shaving any week now.

Well, maybe any month.

She grinned, but only inside her head. "I'm sure," she said.

"There are more exotic hiding places. All those lochs and castles we saw in Scotland..."

Ariane laughed. "Too cliché."

Wally grinned. "I guess you're right."

Ariane looked back out over the lake, the mist rising from it in long tendrils that drifted lazily across the grey surface of the water in the light breeze. "As long as it's in fresh water, I'll feel it," she said. "And no one else can find it. It will be here, but hidden – just like it has been for centuries. Until it's needed."

"Like Arthur, returning in Britain's hour of need," Wally said.

Ariane shot him a smile. "Which he did. Or at least in my hour of need." She knelt down then, and put the old fishing-rod case on the muddy ground at her feet. She opened it, and drew out the sword. It glinted pale gold in the morning light. She stood up, and looked around at the parking lot.

It was silent and deserted. In fact, the whole city seemed to be holding its breath. Even the traffic noise had faded away, as though a bubble of silence surrounded them.

Maybe it does, Ariane thought. *It would hardly be the strangest thing that's happened.*

The sword didn't seem concerned about what she had planned. It was still hers, and knew it, and it didn't matter where it was, as long as it was whole and tied to her magic.

She grinned then, as she thought of something. 'Watch this," she said to Wally.

She reached back, and threw the sword toward the lake.

If she'd had to rely solely on her own muscles, it wouldn't have travelled more than a couple of metres. But Ariane wasn't throwing with her strength alone, but with that of the sword. It flew impossibly far out into the lake, halfway to Willow Island, glinting and glittering as it spun through the misty air. Then Ariane exerted just a little more of her power, and a watery arm, sheathed in white ice, reached up from the lake and caught the sword neatly in its transparent fingers.

For a moment the arm held the sword triumphantly above the glassy surface, and then it withdrew, drawing Excalibur smoothly down into the lake.

From the spot where it had vanished, concentric ripples spread out, smoothed, and then were gone as though they had never been.

Ariane took a deep breath, as though she'd just been relieved of an enormous burden. She picked up the now-empty case with her left hand and offered her right to

Wally. He took it.

"Coffee and a cinnamon bun?" she said.

Wally brightened. "At the Human Bean?"

Ariane laughed. "At the Human Bean."

"Sweet!"

Hand in hand, the Lady of the Lake and the heir of King Arthur turned their back on Wascana Lake and its hidden treasure, and went in search of caffeine and carbs.

THE END

ACKNOWLEDGEMENTS

It's been both a long and yet lightning-fast journey to the conclusion of The Shards of Excalibur. *Song of the Sword* came out just two years ago, yet here we are already at story's end.

My first thanks must go to you, the readers, who have followed Ariane and Wally's fantastical adventures from the beginning. I know you're fond of these characters: I am, too, and hope I've done them justice.

Second, thanks to my excellent editor for the entire series, Matthew Hughes, himself a terrific science fiction and fantasy author: check him out at www.archonate.com.

Third, thanks to everyone at Coteau Books for your great work with design, publicity, and promotion, and especially your enthusiasm for Wally's and Ariane's adventures.

Last but never least, thanks to my wife, Margaret Anne, and daughter, Alice, for understanding that sometimes I live more in the worlds inside my head than the world outside. I love you both more than I can express in words... and I'm pretty good with words.

ABOUT THE AUTHOR

EDWARD WILLETT is the award-winning author of more than fifty science-fiction and fantasy novels, science and other non-fiction books for both young readers and adults, including the acclaimed fantasy series *The Masks of Aygrima*, written under the pen name E.C. Blake.

His science fiction novels include *Lost in Translation*, *Marseguro* and *Terra Insegura*. *Marseguro* won the 2009 Prix Aurora Award for best Canadian science-fiction or fantasy novel.

His non-fiction writing for young readers has received National Science Teachers Association and VOYA awards.

Edward Willett was born in New Mexico and grew up in Weyburn, Saskatchewan. He has lived and worked in Regina since 1988. In addition to his numerous writing projects, Edward is also a professional actor and singer who has performed in dozens of plays, musicals and operas in and around Saskatchewan, hosted local television programs and emceed numerous public events.

BOOKS IN

THE SHARDS OF EXCALIBUR

SERIES:

Book One
Song of the Sword

Book Two
Twist of the Blade

Book Three
Lake in the Clouds

Book Four
Cave Beneath the Sea

Book Five
Door Into Faerie